Unearthed by the master Kafka biographer Reiner Stach and translated by the peerless Michael Hofmann, the seventy-four pieces gathered here have been lost to sight for decades, and two of them have never been translated into English before. Some stories are several pages long; some run about a page; a handful are only a few lines long. All are marvels: even the most fragmentary texts are revelations. These pieces are drawn from the two large volumes of the S. Fischer Verlag edition *Nachgelassene Schriften und Fragmente* (totaling some 1,100 pages).

"'Finished' seems to me, in the context of Kafka, a dubious or ironic condition. Gregor Samsa's sister Grete getting up to stretch in the streetcar. What kind of an ending is that?! Everything continues to vibrate or unsettle, anyway. Reiner Stach points out that none of the three novels were 'completed.' Some pieces break off, or are concluded, or stop—it doesn't matter!—after two hundred pages, some after two lines. The gusto, the friendliness, the wit with which Kafka launches himself into these things is astonishing." —MICHAEL HOFMANN

"Kafka is the greatest German writer of our time. Such poets as Rilke or such novelists as Thomas Mann are dwarfs or plaster saints in comparison to him." —VLADIMIR NABOKOV

REINER STACH *is the author of the definitive, monumental, "superb" (PW) three-volume biography of Kafka. For his translations, the acclaimed poet* MICHAEL HOFMANN *has won countless prizes and been hailed by John Ashbery as "brilliant, stirring, singular."*

The Lost Writings

Also available from New Directions

FRANZ KAFKA
(translated by Michael Hofmann)
Amerika: The Man Who Disappeared
Investigations of a Dog: Stories

REINER STACH
Is That Kafka? 99 Finds

Franz Kafka

The Lost Writings

*selected and
with an afterword
by Reiner Stach*

translated by Michael Hofmann

A NEW DIRECTIONS PAPERBOOK

PUBLISHER'S NOTE: All texts are translated from volume II
of *Nachgelassene Schriften und Fragmente* (S. Fischer Verlag), except
for pp. 3 and 109–128, which are drawn from volume I.

First published clothbound in 2020
Manufactured in the United States of America

Library of Congress Cataloging-in-Publication Data
Names: Kafka, Franz, 1883–1924, author. |
Stach, Reiner, compiler, writer of afterword. |
Hofmann, Michael, 1957 August 25– translator.
Title: The lost writings / Franz Kafka ; selected & with an afterword
by Reiner Stach ; translated by Michael Hofmann.
Description: First edition. |
New York : A New Directions Paperbook, 2020.
Identifiers: LCCN 2020021801 | ISBN 9780811228015 (cloth ;
acid-free paper) | ISBN 9780811228022 (ebook)
Classification: LCC PT2621.A26 A6 2020 | DDC 833/.912–dc23
LC record available at https://lccn.loc.gov/2020021801

10 9 8 7 6 5 4 3 2

New Directions Books are published for James Laughlin
by New Directions Publishing Corporation
80 Eighth Avenue, New York 10011

The Lost Writings

I lay on the ground at the foot of a wall, writhing in agony, trying to burrow down into the damp earth. The hunter stood next to me, pressing his foot gently down on my back. A capital specimen, he said to the driver, already cutting through my jacket and collar to feel me. The dogs, bored with me already and avid for new tasks, were running mindlessly against the wall. The coach arrived, and with hands and legs bound I was tossed next to the gentleman on the back seat, with my head and arms dangling out of the window. The drive was brisk; athirst, with open mouth, I breathed in clouds of dust, and every so often I felt the gentleman greedily pinching my calves.

So, you want to leave me? Well, one decision is as good as another. Where will you go? Where is away-from-me? The moon? Not even that is far enough, and you'll never get there. So why the fuss? Wouldn't you rather sit down in a corner somewhere, quietly? Wouldn't that be an improvement? A warm, dark corner? Aren't you listening? You're feeling for the door. Well, where is it? So far as I remember, this room doesn't have one. At the time this was built, no one had imagined such earth-shattering plans as yours. Well, no matter, a thought like yours won't get lost, we'll discuss it over dinner, and our laughter will be your reward.

A large loaf of bread lay on the table. Father came in with a knife to cut it in half. But even though the knife was big and sharp, and the bread neither too soft nor too hard, the knife could not cut into it. We children looked up at Father in surprise. He said: "Why should you be surprised? Isn't it more surprising if something succeeds than if it fails? Go to bed, perhaps I'll manage it later." We went to bed, but every now and again, at all hours of the night, one or another of us got up and craned his neck to look at Father, who stood there, the big man in his long coat, his right leg braced behind him, seeking to drive the knife into the bread. When we woke up early in the morning, Father was just laying the knife aside and said: "You see, I haven't managed yet, that's how hard it is." We wanted to distinguish ourselves, and he gave us permission to try, but we could hardly lift the knife, whose handle was still almost glowing from Father's efforts, it seemed to rear up out of our grasp. Father laughed and said: "Let it go, I'm going out now, I'll try again tonight. I won't let a loaf of bread make a monkey out of me. It's bound to let itself be cut in the end; of course it's allowed to resist, so it's resisting." But even as he said that, the bread seemed to shrivel up, like the mouth of a grimly determined person, and now it was a very small loaf indeed.

*I can swim as well as the others, only I have a better mem-*ory than they do, so I have been unable to forget my formerly not being able to swim. Since I have been unable to forget it, being able to swim doesn't help me, and I can't swim after all.

Boats glided past. I hailed one. The pilot was a solidly built old man with a white beard. I hesitated a little on the pier. He smiled, and looking at him, I climbed in. He pointed to the far end of the boat, and I sat down there. Only to leap up right away, exclaiming: "Large bats you have here," because some large wings had flapped around my head. "Be quiet," he said, already busy with the boat hook, and we pushed off so hard that I almost fell back onto my seat. Instead of telling the pilot where I wanted to go, I asked him if he knew; from his nodding, he knew. That was a great relief to me, I stretched out my legs and leaned back my head, though always keeping an eye on the pilot, and told myself: "He knows where you want to go; behind that brow of his he knows. And he's dipping his oars into the sea to get you there. And by chance it was him you called out to out of all of them, and you even hesitated before getting on board." With satisfaction I closed my eyes a little, but if I wasn't to see the man I at least wanted to hear him, so I asked: "At your age, you probably shouldn't be working any more. Haven't you any children?" "Only you," he replied, "you are my only child. It's only for you that I'm undertaking this trip, then I will sell the boat and stop working." "You refer to your passengers as children here?" I asked. "Yes," he said, "that's the custom here. And the passengers call us Father in turn." "Curious," I said, "so where's mother?" "There," he said, "in the cabin." I got up and in the little round window of the cabin that was stuck in the middle of the boat I saw a hand stretched out in greeting, and the sharply etched features of a woman framed in a black lace kerchief appeared. "Mother?" I asked with a smile. "If you like—" she said. "But you're so much younger than Father?" I said. "Yes," she said, "much younger, he could be my grandfather, and you my husband." "You know," I said, "it's a strange thing if you're in a boat at night all alone, and suddenly a woman crops up [...]

It's the animal with the long tail, the fox-like tail many yards long. I would love to be able to lay my hand on such a tail, but it's not possible, the animal is in constant movement, and its tail flicks out this way and that. The animal resembles a kangaroo, but unusually in its small, flat, oval, almost human-looking face, only its teeth are expressive, whether it bares or conceals them. Sometimes I have the feeling the animal wants to train me; what other reason could it have for withdrawing its tail from me as I reach out to grab it, and then waiting patiently till I am drawn to it again, only to leap away once more.

The deep well. It takes years for the bucket to reach the top, then in an instant it plummets to the bottom, faster than you can lean down; you think you are still holding it in your hands and already you hear the faraway splash, but you're not even listening.

A farmer stopped me on the highway and begged me to come back to his house with him, perhaps I could help, he'd had a falling out with his wife, and their argument was wrecking his life. He also had some simple-minded children who hadn't turned out well, they just stood around or got up to mischief. I said I would be happy to go with him, but it was doubtful whether I, a stranger, would be able to help him in any way, I might be able to put the children to some useful task, but I'd probably be helpless with respect to his wife, because quarrelsomeness in a wife usually has its origin in some quality in the husband and since he was unhappy with the situation, he had probably already taken pains to change himself but hadn't succeeded, so how could I possibly have more success? At the most, what I could do was divert the ire of the wife to myself. At the beginning, I was speaking more to myself than to him, but then I asked him what he would pay me for my trouble. He said we would rapidly come to some agreement; if I turned out to be of use, I could help myself to whatever I wanted. At that I stopped and said this sort of vague promise was not going to satisfy me, I wanted a precise agreement as to what he would give me per month. He was astonished that I demanded anything like a monthly wage from him. I in turn was astonished that he was astonished. Did he suppose I could fix in a couple of hours what two people had done wrong over the course of their entire lives, and did he expect me at the end of those two hours to take a sack of dried peas, kiss his hand in gratitude, bundle myself up in my rags, and carry on down the icy road? Absolutely not. The farmer listened in silence, with head lowered but tense. The way I saw it, I told him, I would have to stay with him a long time to first become familiar with the situation and think about possible improvements, and then I will have to stay even longer to create proper order, if such a thing was even possible, and by then I will be old and tired and will not be going anywhere but will rest and enjoy the thanks of the parties involved.

"That won't be possible," said the farmer. "Here you are wanting to install yourself in my house and maybe even drive me out of it in the end. Then I would be in even more trouble than I am already." "Unless we trust one another we won't come to an agreement," I said. "Have I not shown I have trust in you? All I have is your word and couldn't you break that? After I'd arranged everything in accordance with your wishes, couldn't you send me packing, for all your promises?" The farmer looked at me and said: "You would never let that happen." "Do what you want," I said, "and think of me as you please but don't forget—I'm saying this to you in friendship, as one man to another—that if you don't take me with you, you won't be able to stand it for much longer in your house. How are you going to go on living with your wife and those children? And if you don't take a chance and take me home with you, then why not drop everything and all the trouble you'll go on having there, and come with me, we'll go on the road together, and I won't hold your suspicions against you." "I'm not at liberty to do that," said the farmer, "I've been living with my wife now for fifteen years, it was difficult, I don't even understand how I did it, but in spite of that I can't just abandon her without having tried everything that might her bearable. Then I saw you on the road, and I thought I might make one final effort with you. Come with me, I'll give you whatever you want. What do you want?" "I don't want much," I said, "I'm not out to exploit your predicament. I want you to take me on as your laborer for life, I can do all sorts of work and will be very useful to you. But I don't want to be treated like other laborers, you're not to give me orders, I have to be allowed to do what work I please, now this, now that, now nothing at all, just as I please. You can ask me to do something so long as you're very gentle about it, and if you see that I don't want to do it, then you'll have to accept the fact. I won't require money, but clothes, linens, and boots up to present standards, and replaced when necessary; if such things are unobtainable in your village, then you'll have to go into town to buy them. But don't worry about that, my present clothes should last me for years. I'll be happy with standard laborers' fare, only I do insist on having meat every day." "Every day?" interjected the farmer, as though satisfied with all the other conditions. "Every day," I said. "I note your teeth are unusual," he said, trying to excuse my unusual stipulation, and he even reached into my mouth to feel them: "Very sharp," he said, "like a dog's." "Well, anyway, meat every day," I said. "And as much in the way of beer and spirits as you." "That's a lot," he said, "I drink a lot." "So much the better," I said, "then if you tighten your belt, I'll tighten mine. Probably you only drink like that because of your unhappy home life." "No," he said, "why should that be connected? But you shall have as much as me, we'll drink together." "No," I said, "I refuse to eat or drink in company. I insist on eating and drinking alone." "Alone?" asked the farmer in astonishment, "all these wishes are making my head spin." "There's not so much," I said, "and I've almost got to the end. I want oil for a lamp that is to be kept burning at my bedside all night. I have the lamp here, just a very little one, it runs on next to nothing. It's really hardly worth mentioning, and I just mentioned it for the sake of completeness, lest there be some subsequent dispute between us; I dislike such things when it comes to being paid. At all other times I am the mildest of men, but if terms once agreed are violated, I cut up rough, remember that. If I am not given everything I have earned, down to the last detail, I am capable of setting fire to your house while you're asleep. But you have no need to deny what we have clearly agreed, and then, especially if you make me the occasional present out of affection, it doesn't have to be worth much, just the odd little trifle, I will be loyal and hardy and very useful to you in all manner of ways. And I shall want nothing beyond what I have told you just now, only on August 24, my name day, a little two-gallon barrel of rum." "Two gallons!" exclaimed the farmer, clapping his hands together. "Yes, two gallons," I said, "it's not so much. You probably think you can beat me down. But I've already reduced my requirements to the bones, out of regard for you of course, I would be ashamed if some stranger were to hear us. I couldn't possibly speak as we have just now in front of a stranger. So no one is to hear of our agreement. Well, who would believe it in any case." But the farmer said, "It's better that you go your own way. I will go on home and try to make things up with the wife. It's true, I have beaten her a lot of late, I think I'll let up a little, perhaps she'll be grateful to me, and I've beaten the children a lot as well, I always get the whip out of the stables and beat them, I'll ease up on that a bit, maybe things will improve. Admittedly, I've tried it in the past without the least improvement. But your demands are too much, and even if they weren't, but no, it's more than the business will bear, not possibly, meat every day, two gallons of rum, even if it had been possible, my wife would never allow it, and if she doesn't allow it, then I can't do it." "So why the long negotiations," I said […]

I loved a girl who loved me back, but I was forced to leave her.

Why?

I don't know. It was as though she was surrounded by a ring of armed men who held out their lances in all directions. No matter how I sought to approach, I encountered their sharp points, was wounded, and had to retire. I suffered badly.

Was the girl in no way responsible?

I don't think so, in fact, I know she wasn't. The above comparison was not the whole story, because I too was ringed by armed men, though they pointed their lances backward, in my direction. As I moved toward the girl, I was immediately caught in the lances of my own men and could make no further progress. It's possible that I never came close to the armed men of the girl, and if I did, then I was already bleeding and insensible from the lances of my own men.

Did the girl remain alone then?

No, another suitor got through to her, easily and unhindered. Exhausted by my own efforts, I watched as indifferently as though I were the air through which their faces met in their first kiss.

I was staying in the Hotel Edthofer, Albian or Cyprian
Edthofer, some name like that, I can't quite remember the whole of it, probably I wouldn't be able to find it again either, even though it was a very large hotel and extremely well appointed and managed. Nor can I remember why, even though I was barely there for a week, I was put to the trouble of changing rooms almost every day, so I often wouldn't know my room number and when I got back during the day or in the evening, I would have to ask the chambermaid which one it was. At least all the rooms that were possible for me were on one floor, and even one corridor. There weren't many of them either, so I didn't have to go looking for long. Was it perhaps just this one corridor that served hotel purposes, while the rest of the building was apartments, something like that? I don't remember, perhaps I didn't even know at the time, it didn't bother me. But it does seem unlikely, since the building had large metal lettering on the front, widely spaced and not very luminous, a sort of reddish-matte metal with the word *Hotel* and the name of the owner. Or was it perhaps just the name of the owner, without the *Hotel*? It's possible, and that might explain something. Even today from my unclear memory, I would think the word *Hotel* was there. Many officers stayed there. Of course, I spent most of my days in the city, I had lots to do and a lot to see so I didn't have time

to observe the hotel scene, but I know I saw a lot of officers there. Agreed, there was a barracks next door, or not really next door, the connection between the hotel and the barracks was somehow different, both looser and tighter. At this distance in time it's not easy to describe, in fact, even then it wouldn't have been easy, I didn't seriously set myself to define the relationship, even though this opacity did sometimes make difficulties for me. Sometimes when I came home at night, with my head bonging with the din of the big city, I was unable to find the hotel entrance right away. It's true, the entrance does seem to have been very small, it's even possible—though this would have been odd—that there was no proper entrance as such, but to go into the hotel you first had to make your way through a restaurant. It may have been that way, but then even the door of the restaurant wasn't always easy to find. Sometimes I thought I was standing in front of the hotel, but I was actually standing in front of the barracks, in a completely different square, quieter and cleaner than the one in front of the hotel, yes, deathly quiet and awesomely clean, but somehow it was able to be taken for the other. Then you had to go around the corner to find yourself in front of the hotel. It seems to me now that sometimes, only sometimes admittedly, you could get from the quiet square—say, with the help of an officer who was going the same way—and find the hotel entrance right away, and not a second or back entrance either, but the one through the restaurant, a narrow and unusually lofty door, covered on the inside by a fine white muslin curtain hemmed with satin ribbon. And all the time, the hotel and the barracks were two perfectly distinct buildings, the hotel lofty in the familiar hotel style, though admittedly with a touch of revenue house about it, while the barracks was low and squat like a sort of Roman castello. The barracks explained the constant presence of so many officers; I never saw any sign of men. I can't remember how I learned that the seeming castello was actually a barracks, but I had occasion to occupy myself with it on frequent occasions, as mentioned above, when angrily looking for the hotel door I wandered around the quiet square. Once I was up in the corridor, however, I was home free. And I did feel very much at home there, happy in the big strange city to have found such a welcoming abode.

There are many waiting here. A vast crowd disappearing into the darkness. What do they want? There are obviously certain demands they want to make. I will listen to them and then make my reply. I will not go out onto the balcony; I couldn't even if I wanted to. In winter the balcony door is kept locked, and the key is somewhere else. Nor will I step up to the window. I will see no one, I will not have my head turned by a spectacle, my desk is the place for me, with my head in my hands, that is my posture.

I was sitting in the box next to my wife. We were watching a rather exciting play, all about jealousy, in a hall of gleaming pillars a man was just raising a dagger to stab his wife as she was walking off. Tensely I leaned over the parapet, against my temple I could feel a lock of my wife's hair. Just then we both shrank back; what we had taken for the velvet upholstered parapet was the back of a long thin man, who, slender as the parapet, had till that point been lying on his front and now turned around to shift his position. My wife clutched me in shock. His face was very near mine, no larger than the palm of my hand, pure and clean as wax, and with a black chin beard. "Why are you alarming us?" I demanded, "what are you doing here?" "Forgive me!" said the man, "I am an admirer of your wife's; the sensation of her elbows in my ribs made me happy." "Emil, please, protect me," cried my wife. "My name is Emil as well," said the man, who propped his head on one hand and lay there as on a chaise: "Come here, little wifey." "You vagabond," I said, "one more word out of you, and you'll be down in the stalls," and, certain this word would be forthcoming, I made to push him down, but it wasn't so easy, he seemed to be part of the parapet, built into it in some way, I wanted to roll him down, but he laughed and said: "Forget it, you fool, don't waste your strength, the fight is only just beginning and it won't end until your wife gratifies my desires." "Never!" exclaimed my wife, and, turning to me: "Please push him off!" "I can't," I cried, "you can see how hard I'm trying, but there's some trick here and I can't." "Oh dear, oh dear," wailed my wife, "what will become of me?" "Calm yourself, please," I said, "your getting excited just makes things worse, I have a new plan: I will take my knife and cut through the velvet upholstery, and tip the whole thing down, along with this man." But then I couldn't find my knife. "Do you know where I put my knife?" I asked, "do you think I left it in my coat pocket?" I was at the point of running down to the cloakroom, when my wife brought me to reason. "You're not about to leave me on my own now are you, Emil?" she cried. "But if I don't have my knife—" I shouted back. "Take mine," she said, and with trembling fingers groped through her little handbag and, of course, produced a tiny mother-of-pearl-handled thing.

A delicate matter, this tiptoeing across a crumbling board set down as a bridge, nothing underfoot, having to scrape together with your feet the ground you are treading on, walking on nothing but your reflection down in the water below, holding the world together with your feet, your hands cramping at the air to survive this ordeal.

What is your complaint, forsaken soul? Why flutter around the house of the living? Why do you not disappear into your distance, instead of fighting here for what is not yours? Rather the living pigeon on the roof than the tenacious sparrow half-dead in the hand.

It is a mandate. It is in my nature that the only mandate I can accept is one that no one has given me. It is in this contradiction, always in a contradiction, that I am able to live. But maybe it's like that for everyone: dying we live, and living we die. Take a circus, it's walled in by canvas, so that no one on the outside can see anything. Now someone finds a little hole in the canvas, and he can see in. Admittedly, his presence there has to be suffered. We all will be suffered in that way for a while. Admittedly—second admittedly—most of what you can see through such a hole is the spectators' backs. Admittedly—third admittedly—you will hear the music and also the roaring of the animals. Until finally, unconscious with terror, you fall back into the arms of a policeman, who for professional reasons has walked around the circus and quietly tapped you on the shoulder to draw your attention to the shameful fact that you have been tensely watching something for which you have not paid.

I was helpless in the face of the form quietly sitting at the table looking at the tabletop. I walked around her and felt she was choking me. A third person was walking around me, feeling choked by me. A fourth walked around the third. And so it carried on to the stars, and beyond. All of us feeling the grip around the throat.

The Count was eating lunch, it was a quiet summer's day.
The door opened, but this time it wasn't the servant, it
was his brother Philotas. "Brother," said the Count, rising to his feet, "imagine seeing you again after years of
not even seeing you in dreams." A pane in the French
window that gave onto the terrace broke in pieces, and
a bird, russet-brown like a pheasant, but larger and
with a longer beak, flapped into the room. "Just a min-
ute, I'll catch it first," said the brother, bunching up his
robe in one hand and grabbing for the bird with the
other. Just then the servant walked in with a splendid
bowl of fruit, which the bird, flying in small circles,
pecked at vigorously.

Rigidly the servant held the bowl and stared with
little semblance of surprise at the fruit, the bird, and
the brother continuing to give chase. Another door
opened, and some villagers entered with a petition,
they were asking for free use of a forest road that
they needed for better access to their fields. But they
had come at an inopportune moment, because the
Count was still a small child, sitting on a stool, doing
his homework. The old Count had admittedly gone
on, and the young one was to have been his heir, but
that's not what happened, there was a lacuna in the
history and so the delegation went knocking into a
void. Where will they end? Will they return? Will they
grasp in time how things stand? The schoolmaster

who was one of their number stepped forward, taking over the tuition of the little Count. With a stick, he pushes everything off the table, which he sets on end like a blackboard, and on it with a piece of chalk writes down the number 1.

To be perfectly honest, I am not very interested in the whole matter. I am lying in a corner, watching, inasmuch as you can see anything from a recumbent position, listening, inasmuch as I am able to understand anything, other than that I have been living in a sort of twilight for months, waiting for night to fall. My cellmate is in a different situation, an adamantine character, a captain. I can imagine his situation. He is of the view that his predicament is like that of a polar explorer who is frozen in some bleak waste but who will surely be rescued, or rather, has already been rescued, as one will be able to read in some account of polar exploration. And now there is the following schism: the fact that he will be rescued is for him beyond doubt, irrespective of his will, simply by virtue of the weight of his victor's personality; now, should he wish for it? His wishing or not wishing will affect nothing, he will be rescued, but the question of whether he ought to wish for it as well remains. It is with this seemingly abstruse question that he is engaged, he thinks it through, he lays it out before me, we discuss it together. We don't talk about his rescue. For the rescue he is apparently content to pin all his hopes on a little hammer he has somehow obtained, the sort of little hammer you use to drive thumbtacks into a drawing board, he cannot afford anything more, but he doesn't use it either, its mere possession delights him. Sometimes he kneels beside me and holds the hammer I've seen thousands of times in front of my face, or he takes my hand, spreads it out on the floor, and hammers all my fingers in turn. He knows that this hammer is not enough to knock the least splinter out of the wall, he doesn't seek to do so either, sometimes he runs his hammer along the walls, as though to give the signal to the great waiting machinery of rescue to swing into operation. It will not happen exactly in this way, the rescue will begin in its own time, irrespective of the hammer, but it remains something, something palpable and graspable, a token, something one can kiss, as one cannot kiss rescue.

Of course, one might say the captain has been driven mad by captivity. The circle of his thinking is so diminished that it barely has room for a single thought.

A rainy day. You are standing over the sheen of a puddle.
Not tired, not sad, not reflective, just standing there in
all your earthly mass, waiting for someone. You hear
a voice whose mere sound, without words, brings a
smile to your face. "Come," says the voice. There is
no one anywhere around for you to go to. "Happily,"
you say, "but I can't see you." Whereupon you hear
nothing further. But the man you had been waiting for
comes, a big strong fellow with small eyes, bushy eye-
brows, thick pendulous jowls and side whiskers. You
have the sense you've seen him somewhere before. Of
course you have, he is your old friend from work, you
arranged to meet him here and talk with him about a
long-looming business matter. But even though he's
standing in front of you with the rain dripping off the
familiar brim of his trusty hat, it's difficult for you to
recognize him. Something is in the way, you'd like to
push it aside, you want to get into conversation with the
man, so you take him by the arm. But straightaway you
let him go again, something disgusts you, what have
you touched? You look at your hand, and even though
you can't see anything you are nauseated. You come
up with some excuse, which probably isn't one, because even as you're saying it, you forget what it is, and
you walk off, straight into a wall—the man calls after
you, perhaps to warn you, you gesture back at him—
the wall opens up before you, a servant is carrying

a candelabrum aloft, and you follow him. Where he leads you is not an apartment but a pharmacy. A large pharmacy with a lofty concave wall studded with a hundred identical drawers. There are plenty of shoppers there as well, most have thin long sticks with which they rap on the drawer from which they want something. Thereupon the assistants scale the wall with tiny speedy climbing motions—you don't see what they're climbing on, you wipe your eyes and still you can't see it—and bring down whatever has been called for. Is it just by way of entertainment or is it part and parcel of the assistants? Either way they have long bushy tails sticking out at the back of their trousers, like squirrels' tails but much longer, and these tails jerk as they climb. Because of the bustle of shoppers streaming this way and that, it's not possible to see how the shop is connected with the street, but you do see a small closed window that probably gives onto the street, to the right of where you think the doorway probably is. Through this window you can make out three individuals who so completely fill the window that it's not possible to say whether the street behind them is jam-packed or deserted. What one principally sees is a man who draws all attention to himself, on either side he is flanked by a woman, but one hardly notices them, they are bowed or sunk or are just slumped against the man, they are completely beside the point, whereas the man, the man himself somehow has a feminine aspect. He is powerfully built, wearing a blue work shirt, his face is broad and open, the nose flattened, it's as though it has just recently been flattened and the nostrils are fighting for their lives, twisting and writhing, the cheeks are full of healthy color. He stares into the pharmacy, moves his lips, cranes left and right as though searching for something. In the shop one man catches the eye who is neither looking for anything nor serving, he walks around perfectly upright, seeking to keep everything in view, pinching his restless lower lip between two fingers, sometimes examining his pocket watch. He is obviously the owner, the shoppers point him out to each other, he is easily identified by numerous long, thin, round leather straps that are looped around him, vertically and horizontally, neither too tight nor too loose. A fair-haired boy of ten or so clutches onto his jacket, and he sometimes reaches for one of the straps as well, he is asking for something that the pharmacist will not give him. The bell rings over the door. Why does it ring? So many customers have come and gone without it ringing, and now it rings. The crowd pushes away from the door, it's as though the ring had been expected, it's even as though the crowd knew more than it admitted. And now one sees the large glazed double door. Outside is a narrow empty alleyway, nicely paved in brick, it's a cloudy gray day, no rain is falling. A gentleman has just opened the door from the alleyway, setting the bell in motion, but now it seems he is doubtful, he takes a step back, he reads the sign of the firm, no, he's come to the right place, and he steps inside. It is Herodias the doctor, and everyone in the crowd knows it. With his left hand in his trouser pocket he walks up to the pharmacist, who is now standing all alone in empty space; even the boy has retreated, albeit only as far as the front row of the spectators, and is watching with blue eyes opened wide. Herodias has a smiling supercilious way of speaking, his head is tipped back, and even when he is speaking he gives the appearance of listening. And yet he is very unconcentrated, some things he needs to be told twice, it's difficult to get through to him, and something is making him smile as well. How should a doctor not know a pharmacy, and yet he looks about him as though he were here for the very first time, and he shakes his head at the sales personnel with their twitching tails. Then he approaches the pharmacist, takes his shoulder with his right hand, turns him around, and now the pair of them make their way through the retreating crowd into the interior of the pharmacy, the boy in front of them, always shyly looking back. Behind the counter they come to a curtain that the boy raises for them, then they proceed through the laboratory rooms and finally reach a small door that, as the boy doesn't dare, the doctor is compelled to open himself. There is a risk that the crowd which has followed them thus far will follow them into the room. But the salespeople, who have made their way into the front row by now, turn against the crowd, not waiting for an order from the gentleman; they are young and well built, but also clever; gently and quietly they push back the crowd, which, incidentally had come after them only by sheer force of numbers, not with any intention. Still, there is now evidence of some countermovement. It is the man with the two women who is responsible for this, he has left his place by the window, has come into the shop, and means to go farther than any of the others. Purely because of the yieldingness of the crowd, which has evident respect for this place, he succeeds. In between the salespeople, whom he thrusts aside more by a couple of quick glances to either side than with his elbows, he, with his female escorts, has approached the two gentlemen, and being taller than they are, peers between their heads into the darkened room. "Who is it?" comes a woman's feeble voice from within. "Be quiet, it's the doctor," replies the pharmacist, and they enter the room. It doesn't occur to anyone to switch on a light. The doctor leaves the pharmacist and approaches the bedside by himself. The man and the women lean against the bedposts at the invalid's feet as if on a balustrade. The pharmacist doesn't dare go farther, and the boy is back at his side. The doctor feels hampered by the presence of the three strangers. In a low voice out of respect for the sick woman, he asks, "Who are you?" "Neighbors," says the man. "What are you doing here?" In a voice much louder than the doctor's, the man says, "We want [...]

I was rowing on a lake. I was in a hollow cave with no daylight, and yet conditions were perfectly bright, a clear even light was shining down from the pale blue rocks. Though there was not a puff of wind, the waves were high, though not so high as to endanger my small but sturdy craft. I rowed calmly through the waves, hardly thinking about my strokes, so intent was I on taking in with all my faculties the silence that reigned here, a silence such as I had never encountered in all my life. It was like a fruit I had never tasted, though it was the most nutritious of all fruits. I had closed my eyes and was drinking it in. Admittedly, I was not undisturbed, the silence might have been absolute, but a disturbance was looming, something still held back the noise, but it was at the door, bursting with a desire to break out. I rolled my eyes against the one who was not there, then pulled an oar out of the oarlock, stood up in the unsteady boat, and brandished my oar at the void. It remained quiet, and I went back to rowing.

The city resembles the sun, all its light is concentrated into one dazzling central circle, you lose your way, you can't find the street or building you're looking for, once you're in there you will never emerge; in a farther, much larger ring things are still compressed, but there is no longer uninterrupted radiation, there are little dark alleyways, discreet passages, even small squares that lie in dimness and cool; beyond, there is an even larger ring where the light is so diffuse that you have to look for it, great blocks of the town stand there in cold gray; and then at last you find yourself in the open country, matte, bare, late autumnal, shot through by the occasional lightning.

It is always very early morning in this city, the sky is a level, barely broken gray, the streets are empty, pure and silent, somewhere an unfixed shutter is slowly stirring, somewhere the ends of a cloth that has been laid over the rail of a balcony on one last story are shifting, somewhere in an open window a curtain is billowing, otherwise there is nothing moving.

If you keep on walking, paddling through the balmy air, your hands by your sides like fins, glimpsing in haste's half-sleep everything you pass by on your way, you will one day let the wagon pass you. Whereas if you stop still, allowing your gaze to put down deep and broad roots, so that nothing can remove you (and yet they are not real roots but only the strength of your purposeful gaze), then you will also see the unchanging dark horizon from which nothing can come, except, on one signal occasion, the wagon, coming trundling up to you, looming ever larger, and at the moment it reaches you it fills the whole world and you sink into it like a child in the upholstery of a railway wagon driving through night and storm.

Twenty little gravediggers, none any bigger than an aver-
age pinecone, form a separate group. They occupy
a wooden barrack-like building in the forest, where
they rest from their arduous labors. There is smoking
there, and shouting and singing, in the usual way of
things when there are twenty workers in one place.
How happy they are! No one pays them, no one equips
them, no one has given them any orders. They have
freely chosen their line of work and they freely perform it. Even in our times, there is still a manly spirit of
can-do. Not everyone would be satisfied by their work,
and perhaps it doesn't quite satisfy them either, but
they don't recoil from their once-taken resolve, they
are used to lugging the heaviest loads through the
densest underbrush. From morning till midnight, the
festive din goes on. Some are telling stories, others are
singing, a few are silently smoking their pipes, but all
pass the great quartern of brandy around the table. At
midnight their leader gets up and bangs on the table,
the men take down their caps from nails, take up rope,
shovels, and pickaxes from the corner, and get into formation, two by two.

Children are all over the church steps as if in a playground,
calling to one another in vulgar terms they of course
do not understand but merely take in their mouths, the
way infants suck on a pacifier. The priest comes out,
brushes the back of his surplice, and sits down on a step.
He wants to calm the children, since their noise is audi-
ble in his church. All he's able to do, however, is pull the
occasional child to himself, the mass eludes him and
continues to play all around him as before. He does not
understand how their game functions, not remotely.
Like balls repeatedly bounced on the ground, they are
hopping and skipping indefatigably and effortlessly on
all the steps and have no more connection than through
their shouts, it's tiring to watch. As though overcome by
sleep, the priest reaches out for the nearest child, a little
girl, undoes the top of her dress—which she requites by
smacking him playfully in the face—sees some signal
he wasn't expecting or perhaps was expecting, exclaims
Aha! pushes the girl away, calls out *Yuck!* and spits and
makes the sign of the cross and gets up to dash back inside. There in the doorway he runs into a young gypsy-
looking woman, she is barefoot, has a red-and-white
patterned skirt and a half-unbuttoned white blouse and
a wild tangle of hair. "Who are you?" he exclaims, his
voice still irate on account of the children. "Emilie, your
wife," she replies softly, and presses herself against his
chest. He is quiet and listens to her heart beat.

41

He gripped his lower lip with his upper teeth, stared into space, and didn't move. "Your behavior is senseless. What's happened to you after all? Your business may not be booming, but it's not terrible either; even if it were to go bust—and there's no question of that— you'll still find it easy to get a start somewhere else, you're young, hale, strong, energetic and have a good grounding, you have only yourself and your mother to look after, so, please, man, get a grip, and tell me why you've summoned me in the middle of the day, sitting there like that?" There was a short pause; I was sitting on the windowsill, he was on a chair in the middle of the room. Eventually he said: "All right, I'll tell you. Everything you said was right but remember this: it's been raining incessantly since yesterday about five o'clock"—he looked at his watch—"it started yesterday and it's still raining at four today. That gives a man something to think about. While it usually rains in the street and not indoors, this time it seems to be the other way around. Look out the window, will you, it's dry outside, isn't it? You see. Whereas in here the water level's rising all the time. Well, let it, let it. It's bad, but I can stand it. With a bit of goodwill, you can stand it, your chair bobs up a little, not too much changes, things bob around and you bob a little higher than they do. It's the rain pattering on my head I can't stand. It may appear to be a detail, but this detail is more

42

than I can stand or perhaps I would be able to except that I feel so helpless in the face of it. And I am helpless, I put on a hat, I open the umbrella, I hold a piece of board over my head, nothing helps, either the rain goes through everything or somewhere just beneath the hat brim, the board, the umbrella, a fresh rain begins just as powerfully."

There was a small pond where we drank, belly and chest on the earth, forelegs, trembling from the bliss of drinking, sunk in the water. Soon we had to go back, though, and the most conscientious of us tore himself free and called: "Brothers, let's return!" And we ran back. "Where were you?" we were asked. "In the woods." "No, you were at the pond." "No, we didn't go there." "Liars, you're still dripping!" And out came the whips. We ran down long passages full of moonlight, here and there one of us was hit and would leap up in the air in agony. The chase finished in the ancestral gallery, where the door was slammed shut, and we were left alone. We were all of us still thirsty, licking the water from our fur and our faces, sometimes instead of water we would find blood on our tongues, that was from the whips [...]

I stood in front of the mine engineer in his office. It was a lean-to on clayey, barely flattened ground. A bare bulb hung down over the middle of his desk. "So, you're looking for work?" said the engineer, propping his forehead in his left hand and in his right holding the pen over a piece of paper. It wasn't a real question, he was just saying it to himself, he was a frail young man of less than medium height, he had to be very tired, his eyes were probably naturally small and narrow, but he gave the appearance of not being able to open them all the way. "Sit down," he said, eventually. But all there was to sit on was a crate, one side of which had been ripped open, from which some ball bearings had issued forth. He had by now detached himself from his desk, only his right hand lay there as before, otherwise he was now leaning back in his chair; his left hand had migrated to his trouser pocket, and he gazed at me. "Who sent you?" he asked. "I read in a technical journal that you were hiring," I said. "I see," he said, with a smile, "so you read that, did you. I must say, you're going about things very crudely." "What do you mean?" I asked, "I don't understand you." "I mean," he said, "that we are not hiring anyone. And if we're not hiring anyone, that means we're not about to hire you either." "All right, all right," I said, angrily getting to my feet. "I didn't really have to sit down to hear that." But then I reflected for a moment and said: "Is there any chance I could stay the night here? It's raining outside, and the village is an hour away." "I don't have any guest rooms here," said the engineer. "Couldn't I stay here, in the office?" "This is where I work, and this—" he pointed to a corner, "is where I sleep." A few blankets and a little straw were indeed piled up there, but then there were also so many other things that I could barely make out that I hadn't so far taken it for a sleeping place.

I am fighting; no one knows it; a few sense it, that's hard to avoid; but no one knows. I perform my daily tasks, I am guilty of some absentmindedness, but not too much. Of course, everyone fights, but I am fighting more than the others, most people fight as though in their sleep, the way you move your hand to dispel a ghost in a dream, whereas I have stepped forward and am fighting with the most detailed and considered use of my forces. What made me step forward out of the rowdy, but in this one respect, troublingly silent crowd? Why have I drawn attention to myself? Why does my name appear on the first page of the enemy's notes? I can't say. A different life didn't seem to me worth living. Born soldiers is what they call such people in books about warfare. But that's not really the case, I am not hoping for victory and I take no delight in fighting for the sake of fighting, the only thing that rejoices me about it is that it's the one thing to do. And as such it rejoices me more than I am in reality capable of appreciating, more than I can give away, perhaps it will be this joy, and not the fighting itself, that will spell my destruction.

Some farm laborers on their way home at night found an old collapsed figure of a man in a ditch by the side of the road. He was mumbling to himself, with eyes half-shut. At first it seemed to be a drunk, but he wasn't drunk. Nor did he seem to be ill either, or weakened by hunger, or exhausted from walking, at least he shook his head in reply to all such questions. "So, who are you?" they finally asked him. "I am a great general," he said, without looking up. "I see," they said, "so that's your trouble, is it." "No," he said, "I really am." "Of course," they said, "how could you be anything else." "You can laugh if you want," he said, "I won't punish you." "We're not laughing," they said, "you can be whatever you like, you can be a field marshal for all we care." "That's what I am," he said, "I'm a field marshal." "You see," they said, "we're on to you. Now never mind us, we just wanted to tell you that it'll freeze tonight and that you can't stay here." "I've got nowhere to go, and I wouldn't know where I would go."

"Why can't you go somewhere?"

"I can't, I don't know why. If I could, I'd be a general in the midst of my army in a trice."

"I suppose they threw you out, did they?"

"Me, a general? No, I fell."

"Fell from where?"

"From the heavens."

"From up there?"

48

"Yes."

"Is that where your army is, then?"

"No. But you're asking too many questions. Go away and leave me here."

A   *"Be honest! When will you next have the chance to sit* cozily over a beer with someone who's listening to you as today? Be honest now! Where does your power reside?"

B   "Do I have power? What sort of power do you mean?"

A   "You're avoiding the issue. You're a dishonest spirit. Maybe your power resides in your disingenuousness."

B   "My power! Because I'm sitting in this little bar, and I have an old schoolmate sitting with me, that makes me powerful."

A   "Then try it this way. Do you think you're powerful? But be honest now, otherwise I'll get up and go home. Do you think you're powerful?"

B   "Yes, I think I'm powerful.

A   "Well then."

B   "But that's purely my concern. No one can see a crumb of that power, not a trace, not even I."

A   "But still you think you're powerful. So wherein does your power reside?"

B   "It's not quite correct to say that I think myself powerful. That's an exaggeration. I, sitting here, old, dirty, and run down, do not think of myself as powerful. The power I believe in is not a power I exercise but others, and they do so by yielding to me. Of course, that can be very shaming for me and not at all glorious. Either I am their servant, whom in a fit of seigneurial good mood they have set above themselves as their master, that would just about be all right, then everything would be a matter of appearances, or again I really have been called upon to be their master, then what am I to do, poor helpless old man that I am? I can't raise a glass to my lips without trembling, and now I'm meant to direct thunderstorms or oceans."

A   "Now see how powerful you are, and you wanted to suppress all that. But we know you. Even if you sit in a corner by yourself, all the regulars know you."

B   "Well, yes, the regulars know plenty, I hear only a fraction of their talk, but what little I hear is my only instruction and encouragement."

A   "What?! You claim to rule on the basis of what you hear?"

B   "No, certainly not. But you belong to those who believe I rule?"

A   "Didn't you just say so?"

B   "How could I have just said so? No, all I said is that I think I am powerful, but I don't exercise my power. I can't exercise it, because my assistants are already there but not yet in position, and they never will be. They are skittish, they hang around everywhere they have no business to be, from all quarters their eyes are on me, and I nod with approval at everything they do. So, was I not right in saying I had no power? And don't call me disingenuous."

"Of what does your power consist?"

"Do you take me for powerful?"

"I take you for extremely powerful, and almost as much as your power I admire the unselfish forbearance with which you use it, or rather the determination with which you deploy your power against yourself. Not content with forbearance, you even fight against yourself. I don't ask why you do such a thing, that is your own deep secret, all I ask about is the source of your power. I think I am entitled to ask because I have recognized your power as not many have, and that its mere threat—which today is almost all that's left of it as a result of your self-discipline—feels like something irresistible to me."

"Your question is easily answered: my power rests in my two wives."

"Your wives?"

"Yes. You've met them, haven't you?"

"Do you mean the women I saw yesterday in your kitchen?"

"Yes."

"Those two fat women?"

"Yes."

"Those women. I hardly paid them any attention. They looked, forgive my saying so, like two cooks. And they were not quite clean, and scruffily dressed as well."

"Yes, that's them."

"Well, if you say so, I believe you, only you've now become even more of a mystery to me than you were before I was told of the two wives."

"It's no mystery. It's plain to see. Let me try and tell you. So, I live with these two women, you saw them in the kitchen, though they rarely cook for me, we usually send out for food from the restaurant opposite, sometimes Resi gets it, and sometimes Alba. No one's actually opposed to cooking at home, but it's too difficult because the two of them don't get along, or rather they get along beautifully but only when they can exist side by side in calm. For example, they can lie together on the narrow sofa for hours without sleeping, which given their girth is no mean feat. But they bicker when there is work to be done, then they quarrel, and they start hitting each other. And so we came to the understanding—they are very amenable to reason and good sense—that they should do as little work as possible. Which further accords with their nature. They think they have tidied the apartment when actually it's so dirty that the first step I take across the threshold disgusts me, but then once I've taken it, I adjust.

"Along with work, every pretext for strife has disappeared. Jealousy in particular is something they are quite unacquainted with. How should they be jealous? I can barely tell them apart. Maybe Alba's nose and lips are a little more negroid than Resi's, but sometimes I have the opposite impression. Maybe Resi has less hair than Alba—she does have disgracefully little hair—but do I make anything of it? I promise you, I can barely tell them apart.

"Also, I only get home from work in the evening, the only time I see them in the daytime is on Sundays. So, I get home late, as I like to wander around by myself after work. For reasons of economy, we don't use the light very much. I can hardly afford to, keeping those two women, who seem to be capable of eating continuously, uses up almost my whole salary. So, I come to the dark apartment and ring the bell. I hear them come puffing up to the door. Resi or Alba says: 'It's him,' and then the puffing gets a little louder. If there were a stranger at the door, he might very well be alarmed.

"Then they open the door, and I usually play the joke on them of forcing myself through the crack and grabbing them by the throat. 'Ooh you' says one of them, which means 'You are incredible,' and then they both laugh their deep, throaty laughs. From that moment on, they are entirely occupied with me, and if I didn't twist a hand free to shut the door, I'm sure it would remain open all night.

"Then the way through the anteroom, no more than a couple of paces though it takes us perhaps the better part of an hour, along which they carry me almost bodily. I am tired, of course, at the end of a hard day, and sometimes I permit my head to drop on Resi's soft shoulder and sometimes on Alba's. They are both almost naked, just wearing little shifts, as they do all day long, except when company is expected, like your visit the other day, when they slip into a few dirty rags.

"Then we reach my room and generally what they do is push me in while they stay outside and shut the door on me. It's a game, because now they start fighting over which of them is allowed in first. This isn't jealousy, though, not a real fight, it's just a game. I listen to the loud gentle blows they exchange, the snorts that now signify actual shortage of breath, the occasional word. Finally, I open the door myself and they plunge in, heated, with torn shifts and the acrid smell of their breathing. We fall down onto the carpet and gradually quiet down."

"But why are you quiet now?"

"I've lost the thread. What was it now? You were asking me about the source of my alleged power, and I told you it was these women. Well, that's the way it is, these women are the source of my power."

"Your merely living with them?"

"My merely living with them."

"You've become monosyllabic."

"You see, my power has limits. Something is telling me to be quiet. Goodbye."

Some people approached me and asked me to build them a city. I said there were not nearly enough of them, they could fit into a single house, why should I build them a city. They replied that others would come after them, and there were married couples among them who would be having children, also the city didn't have to be built all at once, but perhaps just sketched, and then it could be built by and by. I asked them where they wanted their city built, and they offered to show me the place. We walked along the river till we came to a sufficiently elevated plane, steeply shelving down toward the river but wide and flat in all other directions. They said they wanted their city built up there. There was nothing growing but sparse grass, no trees, which I liked, but the slope down to the river struck me as too steep, and I pointed this out to them. They replied that this didn't matter, the city could spread out in other directions and have sufficient access to fresh water, also over the course of time ways might be found to reduce the angle of the decline, at any rate, that wasn't to be an impediment to the founding of the city on this spot. Also, they were young and strong and could easily scramble up and down the incline, as they proceeded to show me. Like lizards they beetled up through the rocks, and they were up at the top in no time. I walked up after them and asked what made them want their city precisely here. The place didn't seem particularly defensible, the only natural boundary was on the river side, where one needed it least, what would have been preferable at that point was an easy access; whereas from every other side their plateau was easily reached, and for that reason, and for its wide extension, difficult to defend. Moreover, they had not had the soil tested for its richness, and to be so dependent on lower ground and vehicular traffic was always a risky thing for a city, especially in these turbulent times. Nor had it been proven that there was any source of drinking water up here, the one stream they showed me hardly seemed adequate to that purpose.

"You're tired," one of them said, "you don't want to build our city." "I am indeed tired," I said and sat down on a rock beside the stream. They dipped a cloth in the water and I thanked them and refreshed my face with it. Then I said I wanted to take a walk around the plateau by myself and left them: it turned out to be a long way; by the time I returned it was already dark, and they were lying by the stream sleeping; a mild rain was falling.

I decided to leave them and climbed down the slope back to the river. But one of them awoke and he awakened the others and then they were all clustered around the edge, and I was only halfway down, and they begged me and called out to me. So I turned back, and they helped me and pulled me up. That was when I promised to build them their city. They were very grateful, gave speeches in my honor, kissed me, [...]

We were walking on smooth ground, sometimes one of us would stumble and fall, sometimes one would almost fall over sideways, then the other had to help, but carefully because his own footing wasn't the best. Finally we came to a hill called the Knee, but even though it's not a big hill we couldn't climb it, we kept slipping off, we were at our wit's end, so now we had to go around it since we couldn't climb over it, which might be just as impossible, but much more dangerous, because failure here meant a fall and the end. We decided, so as not to hamper each other, to make the attempt from different sides. I threw myself down on the ground and slowly pushed myself to the edge; I could see no semblance of a path, no possibility of a hold anywhere, everything fell straight down into the depths. I was certain I wouldn't make it, perhaps conditions on the other side were a little easier, but I'd have to try it to find out, and then we'd both be finished. But we had to take the chance, we couldn't stay here, and behind us bleakly and inaccessibly soared the five sharp peaks called the Toes. I surveyed the scene once more, the stretch, not really all that long, but impassible, and shut my eyes—keeping them open would only have hurt me here—firmly resolved not to open them unless the impossible happened and I did get across to the other side after all. And then I let myself slowly sink to the side, almost as in sleep, stopped, and began to advance. I had extended my arms far ahead and to both sides, this covering and so to speak containing as much area as possible around me seemed to give me a little balance, or more correctly, a little comfort. But then to my own surprise I noticed that this ground was somehow helpful to me. Yes, it was smooth and there was nothing to hold on to, but it wasn't cold, some sort of warmth flowed from it to me, there was a connection that didn't come through my hands and feet but that persisted and held.

"It is not a barren wall, it's living sweetness pressed into a wall, bunches of grapes pressed together."—"I don't believe it."—"Taste it."—"I'm too incredulous to lift a hand."—"I'll put a grape to your mouth, then."— "I won't be able to taste it from incredulity."—"Then drop!"—"Didn't I tell you the barrenness of this wall is enough to lay a man out?"

"You never draw water from the depths of this well."
    "What water? What well?"
    "Who is asking?"
    Silence.
    "What silence?"

No one slept, there was no sleeping in the caravansary; but if no one slept, why did anyone even come here? To rest the animals. It was just a small place, a tiny oasis, but it was completely full of the caravansary, which, one has to say, was enormous. For a stranger, such was my impression, it must be impossible to orient oneself. The type of the construction was partly responsible. You entered the outer courtyard, and from there two arches roughly ten yards apart led into a second courtyard, you passed through an archway, and then, far from being, as expected, in a further large expanse, you found yourself in a dark little space with walls reaching up into the heavens, it was only way up that you saw some illuminated balconies. So you thought you had taken a wrong turn and wanted to return to the first courtyard, and chanced not to go back through the arch you had entered by but the one next to it. Only to find you weren't in the original courtyard at all, but in a different one, much larger, full of music and noise, and the lowing and bleating of animals. You had made a mistake, so you went back into the dark little courtyard and then through the first archway. It was no use, again you were in the second courtyard, and you had to ask for directions through a whole series of other courtyards before you were back in the original courtyard, which it had taken you just a few steps to leave. What was unpleasant was that the first courtyard was always crowded, it was almost impossible to find a place to rest. It almost looked as though the apartments in the first courtyard were full of regular long-term guests, though this couldn't actually be the case, for it was only caravans that put up here, who else could or should have wanted to stay here, the little oasis had nothing but water to offer, and it was many miles from other, bigger oases. No one could live or want to live here unless it might be the owner of the caravansary and his employees, but, though I've stayed there several times, I have yet to see or hear anything of them. It would have been difficult to imagine, had there been a proprietor there, such disorder, yes, including actual violence, being tolerated, as happened here day and night. Rather, I had the impression that the most numerous caravan on any given occasion prevailed, and then the others in order. Even this doesn't explain everything, though. For instance, the large front gate was usually kept locked, opening it for caravans to enter or leave was an elaborate process that took considerable organization. Often the caravans were kept waiting outside for many hours in the burning sun before they were admitted. This was nothing but the most blatant chicanery; however, there seemed to be no solution to it. So they stood outside and had plenty of time to inspect the setting of the ancient gate. Around the gate in two or three rows were angels in relief blowing fanfares, at the apex of the gate one such instrument hung down far into

63

the gateway. The pack animals had to be carefully led around this on each occasion so that they didn't collide with it, given the run-down condition of the building as a whole, it was noticeable that this rather beautiful piece of work had not suffered any damage. Perhaps it was a question of [...]

"You are forever speaking of death, and not dying."

"And yet die I shall. I am just intoning my swan song. One person's song is longer, another's shorter. The only difference is a few words."

It was no prison cell, because the fourth wall was com-
pletely open. The notion that this wall would be or
might be bricked up was appalling, because then,
given the dimensions of the space, which was a yard
deep and only just above head height, I would be in
a sort of vertical stone coffin. Well, for now it wasn't,
I could stretch out my hands, and when I gripped an
iron bracket that hung down from the ceiling, I could
even cautiously put my head out, but cautiously, because I didn't know the elevation of my cell over the
ground. It seemed to be very high up, at any rate I
could see only a gray haze in the depths, the same as
on either side, only it seemed to thin out a little higher
up. It was the sort of perspective you might have from
a tower on an overcast day.

I was tired, and sat down on the edge, letting my feet
dangle. What was annoying was that I was completely
naked, otherwise I might have knotted together some
garments, fastened them to the ceiling bracket, and let
myself down from my cell as far as I could, to see what
I could see. On the other hand, it was probably just as
well that I couldn't, because in my restlessness I might
have done it, with possibly catastrophic results. Much
better to have nothing and do nothing.

In the cell, which was otherwise completely empty
and had bare walls, there were two holes in the floor at
the back. The hole in one corner seemed to be a sort of

66

lavatory, the hole in the other corner had in it a piece of bread and a small, sealed wooden barrel of water, so that was where I was being fed.

*People are individuals, and fully entitled to their individu-*ality, though they must first be brought to an acceptance of it. It was my experience, though, that every effort was made, at school and at home, to expunge any individuality. This made it easier to educate the child, and made its life easier for it, though it meant acquainting it early with pain and duress. An example: no one will ever be able to reason a child into putting down his book and going to bed. When I was told that it was late and I was ruining my eyes, and I would be tired and unable to get up in the morning, and that the silly story wasn't worth the trouble, then I couldn't refute such an argument point by point—mostly because it wasn't even worth considering. Every one of the terms here was endless or so divided and subdivided that it might as well be: time was endless, so it couldn't be too late; my eyesight was endless, so that I couldn't ruin it; even night was endless, so there was no need to worry about getting up; and anyway my criterion for books wasn't whether they were sensible or silly but whether they gripped me or failed to grip me, and this one, whatever it was, gripped me. Of course, I had no way of saying all this, and the upshot was either that I made trouble for myself by pleading to be allowed to go on anyway, or else I decided to go on without permission. So much for my own individuality. It was suppressed by turning off the gaslight and

leaving me in the dark. All I was told by way of explanation was: everyone needs to go to sleep, and it's time
for you to go to sleep. I saw it and had to believe it, even
though it made no sense to me. No one has as much
reforming zeal as children. But quite apart from the
somehow remarkable degree of oppression, in almost
every case there remained a thorn whose sharp prick
could not be blunted by any appeal to principle. I was
left in the belief that on that particular evening no one
in the world had such a desire to read as I did. No appeal to general rules could convince me otherwise, the
less so because I saw that my insuperable desire to read
was not even credited. Only gradually and much later,
maybe as the wish was already waning, did I begin to
believe that many others might have a similar desire,
and they got over it. At the time, though, I only felt the
injustice done to me. I went sadly to sleep, and there
began to develop in me the hatred that has determined
my life within the family and the whole of my life sub-
sequently. Forbidden reading is just one instance, but
it is indicative, because I was deeply touched by it. My
individuality was not respected; but because I could
sense it in myself, I was forced to see—and I was very
sensitive in this, and always on the qui vive—a form
of condemnation in this behavior to me. If my pub-
licly displayed form of individuality was condemned,
then how much worse was it with the other forms that
I kept concealed because I could see that there was
some element of wrongness in them. For instance, if I

had been reading without first having done my home-work. This might be very bad as a form of dereliction of duty, but then I wasn't concerned with such abso-lute judgments, I was only interested in comparative judgments. Faced with such judgment, this dereliction was probably not worse than the long time spent read-ing, especially as it was so limited in its consequences by my great fear of school and authorities; whatever I might on occasion have skimped through reading, I was easily able to make up for the next morning and in school, thanks to my memory, which at the time was excellent. The main thing, though, was that I was now prosecuting the condemnation of my habit of lengthy reading by myself through the further, con-cealed habit of dereliction of duty, which led me to the most crushing result. It was as though someone is to be grazed with a rod that is said not to cause any pain, instead of which he takes the woven ends apart, pulls the individual ends into himself, and following his own plan starts to scratch and stab his flesh, all the while he continues to hold the rod steady in his other hand. If I wasn't yet inflicting grave punishment on myself in these situations, it is nevertheless a certainty that I never accepted any real gain from my individual-ity that would ultimately express itself in the form of self-confidence. Rather, the consequence of a display of willfulness was that I either ended up hating the oppressor or failed to acknowledge the willfulness, two consequences that might go on to be associated in mendacious fashion. If I kept my wilfulness hidden, then the consequence was that I hated either myself or my fate and took myself for wicked or damned. The relationship of these clusters of wilfulness has undergone changes over the years. Public displays of wilfulness became increasingly evident, as my life opened out before me. But they didn't bring me any relief, just as the quantity of what remained hidden from sight was not diminished, rather, it turned out on closer inspection that it was impossible to admit everything; even the seemingly full confessions of earlier times showed the roots of the evil still embedded inside me. Even if it had been otherwise—with the relaxing of the entire inner economy that I have gone through without any decisive interventions, one concealed bit of wilfulness could so shake me that, for all my conformity in other respects, I was unable to grab a hold anywhere. Things got worse. Even if I had kept nothing secret, but had thrown everything as far from me as I could, and was standing there all pure again, the very next moment I would be convulsed with the old confusion because to my way of thinking the secret would not have been fully seen and assessed but returned, given back to me by the generality. This was no deception, but a special form of understanding that says that at least among the living it is not possible for anyone to reject his entire being. If, for instance, someone owns up to his friend that he is a miser, then in that instant he has apparently detached himself from his miserliness for the friend, who is a representative observer. For that instant the friend's reaction is a matter of indifference, whether he denies the existence of the miserliness, or offers advice on how to get free of it, or even seeks to defend it. It might not even matter terribly if the friend in consequence ends the friendship. All that matters is that one has opened oneself up to the generality as an honest, if not a guilty, sinner and thereby hopes to have reacquired the goodness and—this is the part that matters—the freedom of childhood. But all that one has acquired is a brief moment of folly and much subsequent bitterness. Because somewhere on the table, between the miser and the friend, lies the money that the miser must have, and toward which he moves his hand ever more quickly. Halfway there, his admission is weaker but still enough to absolve him; any time after it is not. On the contrary, it merely illuminates the rapidly moving hand. Effective confession is only possible before or after the deed, the deed will not tolerate anything but itself; for the hand clawing at coins and notes there is no absolution by word or feeling, either the act, and in this case the hand, must be destroyed or one persists in miserliness.

"How did I get here?" I exclaimed. It was an averagely large hall softly lit by electric light whose walls I was pacing off. The room had doors, but if you opened them, you found yourself facing a dark wall of sheer rock barely a hand's breadth from the threshold, and running straight up and to either side, as far as one could see. There was no way out there. One door opened into another room, where prospects were perhaps a little more encouraging, but just as strange. You could see into a princely chamber dominated by red and gold, with several tall mirrors and a large crystal chandelier. Nor was that all.

I arrived out of breath. There was a pole jammed into the ground, a little askew, bearing a sign with the legend HOLLOW. I had arrived, I said to myself, and I looked around. A few steps away was a discreet and rather overgrown arbor, from where I could hear a sound of clattering plates. I went there, poked my head through the low opening, saw next to nothing in the dark interior, but said hello anyway and inquired: "Would you happen know who is looking after the hollow?" "At your service, I am," came the friendly reply, "I'll be along in a moment." Gradually I was able to make out the small group within, there was a young couple, three small children who were barely the height of the table, and a babe in arms. The man, who was sitting at the back of the arbor, was on the point of getting up and going out, but his wife told him sweetly to finish his dinner first, at which he gestured in my direction, and she remarked that I would surely have the goodness to wait a little and do them the honor of sharing their frugal lunch with them, till finally, very annoyed with myself for having disturbed their Sunday quiet, I felt compelled to say: "Sadly, sadly, madam, I am unable to comply, because I must immediately, and I mean immediately, have myself lowered into the hollow." "Oh, dear," said the woman, "on a Sunday of all days, and at lunchtime too. People and their whims. They are such slave drivers." "Don't be cross with me,"

I said, "I'm not asking your husband just for the sake of it, and if I knew how it was done, I would long since have done it by myself." "Don't listen to her," said the man, now standing at my side and drawing me away. "Don't expect a woman to understand anything."

"Remarkable!" said the dog, passing his hand over his brow. "All the many places I've been, first across the market square, taking the logging road up the hill, then criss-crossing the plateau, down the defile, along the paved road for a bit, left down to the stream and along the line of poplars, past the church, and now here. Why did I do it? I'm at my wit's end. Just as well I'm back here now. I do so dread this pointless running around, these vast empty spaces, what a poor, helpless, lost dog I am there. It's not even that I'm tempted to run away, this yard is my place, here is my kennel, here is my chain for the odd time I've bitten someone, I have everything here and plenty to eat. So then. I would never run away from here of my own free will, I feel well looked after here, I'm proud of my job, a pleasant sensation of seniority passes through me when I see the other animals. But does any one of them run off as foolishly as I do? Not one, except maybe the cat, that soft, scratchy thing that no one needs and no one misses, she has her secrets that leave me cold, and she runs around in the performance of some duty, but only within the confines of the house. So I am the only one who occasionally goes AWOL, and it's a habit that might one day cost me my senior position. Luckily, no one seems to have noticed today, though only recently Richard, the master's son, passed a remark. It was a Sunday, Richard was sitting on the bench

smoking, I was lying at his feet, with my jowl pressed to the ground. 'Caesar,' he said, 'you bad dog, where were you this morning? I went looking for you at five o'clock, a time when you're still supposed to be on guard, and I couldn't find you anywhere, it wasn't till a quarter to seven that you got in. That's a serious dereliction of duty, you know that?' So I'd been caught out that time. I got up, sat by him, put my arm around him, and said: 'Dear Richard, let me off just this once, and don't tell anyone. It won't happen again if I have anything to do with it.' And for all sorts of reasons—despair at my own nature, fear of punishment, emotion at Richard's kindly expression, joy at the momentary absence of any implement of chastisement—I wept so much that I wet Richard's jacket, and he shook me off, telling me: *Lie down!* So then I'd promised betterment yet today the exact same thing happens, and I was gone for even longer. Admittedly, I only promised I would better myself if it had anything to do with me. And it's not my fault […]

A friend I hadn't seen for many years now, more than twenty, and from whom I heard only occasional news, sometimes nothing for years on end, was returning to our city, his father's city. Since he had no living relatives, and of his friends I was by far the closest to him, I had offered him the use of a room in my apartment and was happy that he had accepted my invitation. I was careful to furnish the room in my friend's taste, trying to remember his particularities, the special wishes he had occasionally expressed, especially during holidays we'd taken together, tried to remember what he had particularly liked and disliked in his surroundings, tried to picture in detail what his boyhood room had looked like, but, of all of that, I succeeded in finding nothing that I could do to my apartment to make him feel any more welcome there. He came from a large poor family: hunger and din and argument had characterized that apartment. In my mind's eye I could exactly see the room off the kitchen where sometimes—on rare occasions—we were able to retreat while the rest of the family squabbled in the kitchen as usual. A small dark room with the permanent pungent smell of coffee, because the door to the even darker kitchen stood open night and day. There we would sit by the window that opened onto a sort of enclosed winter garden that ran around the yard, playing games of chess. There were two pieces missing in our set, and we were forced to replace them with trouser buttons, which caused occasional confusion when we disagreed about their value, but on the whole we had grown accustomed to the substitution and kept faith with it. The neighbor along the passage was a seller of liturgical clothing, a merry but restless man with long drooping mustaches he would finger like a flute. When this man came home in the evening, he had to pass our window, where he would usually stop, lean into the room, and watch us play. He was almost invariably critical of our play, both mine and my friend's, and gave us tips, and he ended up picking up the pieces and moving them, which we had to accept, because if we made to take them back, he would bat away our hands; for a long time, we endured his interventions because he was a better player than either of us, not much better, but sufficiently so that we could learn from him, but on one occasion, when it was already dark, and he was leaning over us, and took the entire board away and set it down on the windowsill to inspect the state of the game, then I got up, having been enjoying a significant advantage in this game and seeing it set at risk by his coarse intervention, and said, with the unthinking rage of the small boy who suffered an evident injustice, that he was disturbing our game. He looked at us briefly, picked up the board, and with an ironic display of care set it down in its former place, walked off, and from that day forth would have nothing to do with us. Only, each time he passed the window, no longer bothering to look inside, he made a dismissive gesture with his hand. To begin with, we celebrated the episode as a huge triumph, but after a while we started to miss him with his instruction, his humor, his willingness to participate, and not knowing why, we started to neglect our games, and before long our interest turned to different things altogether. We began collecting stamps, and it was, as I only understood later, the sign of our almost mystifyingly close friendship that we shared an album. One night I would keep it, the next it was his. The difficulties that resulted from this shared ownership were exacerbated by the fact that my friend was banned from our apartment, my parents would not allow him in. This ban was not originally directed against him—my parents hardly knew him—but against his parents and the rest of his family. In that general way it was probably not unjustified, but in the form it took it wasn't very sensible, as it led directly to my going around to my friend's every day and being drawn far more deeply into the web of that family than if my friend had been permitted to visit us. Often in place of sense my parents offered tyranny, not just toward me but toward the whole of the world. In this case it was enough for them—and here my mother was more deeply involved than my father—that the family of my friend was being punished and degraded. That I was thereby caused to suffer, yes, that in a natural countermeasure my friend's parents treated me with mockery and contempt, this my parents did not know, but then they weren't interested in me in that way, and even if they had gotten to hear of it, they wouldn't have been greatly affected. This is my view of it after the events, at the time we two friends were reasonably content with how things stood and the grief at the imperfection of earthly arrangements did not pierce us, yes, carting the album back and forth daily was irksome, but [...]

From a bar came the sound of singing, a window was open, it wasn't fastened and was swaying back and forth. It was a little single-story hut, and there was nothing around about, it was a long way outside of town. A late customer came slinking along, on tiptoe, in a tight-fitting suit, feeling his way as though in the dark, even though there was a moon. Listened in at the window, shook his head, didn't understand how such beautiful singing could be coming out of such a bar, swung himself in backward over the windowsill, probably a little recklessly, because he lost his balance and fell into the building, but not a long way, because there was a table by the window. The wineglasses fell to the ground, the two men who had been sitting at the table leapt up and swiftly chucked the new customer—whose feet were still outside—back through the window, he landed in soft grass, got up and listened, but by then the singing had stopped.

I was stuck in an impenetrable thicket of thorns and called out to a park warden. He came right away but was unable to reach me. "How did you wind up in the middle of a thicket?" he called to me. "Couldn't you find the same way back?" "Not possible," I called, "I'll never find the way. I went for a walk and was lost in thought, and suddenly found myself here, it's as though the bushes only grew after I got here. I'll never make it out, I'm lost." "You're like a child," said the warden, "first you follow some forbidden path through the worst sort of tangle, and then you start wailing. You're in a public park, not some jungle, and we'll get you out all right." "A thicket like this has no business in a park," I said, "and how do you mean to rescue me, no one can get in here. But if they want to try, then they should do it soon, it's evening now, I'll never survive the night, I'm already scratched up by thorns, and I've lost my pince-nez and I can't find it, I'm half-blind without it." "That's all well and good," said the warden, "but you'll have to show a little patience, I'll have to find some workmen who will hack their way through, and before that I'll need to get the agreement of the park director. So, let's have a little patience and a little manliness, if you please."

We had a visitor whom I had often seen before without endowing him with any particular significance. He went into the bedroom with my parents, they were quite captivated by his conversation and absentmindedly closed the door after them; when I made to follow, Frieda the cook held me back, I of course lashed out and cried, but Frieda was the strongest of the cooks that I can remember, and she was able to press my hands together in an unbreakable grip, at the same time holding me a long way from her, so that I couldn't kick her. After that I was helpless and could only scold. "You're like a dragoon," I screamed. "You should be ashamed of yourself, you're a girl and you're just like a dragoon." But there was no way I could get her excited, she was a placid, almost melancholy thing. She let me go when Mother came out of the bedroom to fetch something from the kitchen. I grabbed hold of Mother's skirts. "What does the man want?" I asked. "Oh," she said, and kissed me, "nothing much, he just wants us to go away together somewhere." That made me very happy, because it was much nicer in the village where we always spent the holidays than it was in the city. But then Mother explained to me that I couldn't come along, I had to go to school, winter was coming and there weren't any more holidays, also they weren't going up to the village at all, but to another city, much farther away, and then she corrected herself, no, not much farther, actually much closer than the village. When I refused to believe her, she took me over to the window and said this other city was so close you could almost see it from the window, but that wasn't true, certainly not on this overcast day, when we couldn't see any more than we could normally: the little alley below, and the church opposite. Then she let me go, went into the kitchen, came back with a glass of water, motioned to Frieda, who was about to launch herself at me again, not to, and pushed me into the bedroom ahead of her. There was Father, tired, sitting in the comfy chair, putting out his hand for the water. On seeing me, he smiled and asked what I would say if they went away somewhere. I said I would love to go with them. He said that I was still too small, and that it was a very strenuous journey. I asked why they had to go at all. My father pointed to the gentleman. The gentleman had golden buttons on his jacket that he was just burnishing with his handkerchief. I asked him to leave my parents here, because if they went away I'd have to stay behind on my own with Frieda, and that was impossible […]

I was allowed to set foot in a strange garden. There were a few obstacles to be negotiated, but finally a man half arose behind a small table and pinned a dark green token in my buttonhole. Our eyes met, and it was agreed that I could now go in. But after a few steps, I remembered that I hadn't paid yet. I wanted to turn back, when I saw a large lady in a traveling coat in some coarse-woven yellow-gray material also standing by the table and counting out a number of tiny coins on the table. "That's for you," called the man, who had probably noticed my disquiet, over the head of the woman, who was bending far down. "For me?" I said disbelievingly, and turned around to see if someone else wasn't meant instead. "Always so persnickety," said a gentleman crossing a piece of lawn, slowly fording the path in front of me, and proceeding onto another bit of lawn. "For you. Who else? People here pay for one another." I was grateful for this albeit unwillingly communicated bit of information but pointed out to the gentleman that I had yet to pay for anyone myself. "Who could you ever pay for?" asked the gentleman, turning to go. I wanted to wait for the lady and attempt to come to an agreement with her, but she went a different way, rustling along in her coat, a blueish veil fluttering behind her powerful form. "That's Isabella you're admiring" said a walker at my side, also watching her pass. And a moment later again: "Isabella."

It is Isabella, the old dapple-gray horse, I hadn't recognized her in the crowd, she's a lady now, the last time we met was at a charity fete in a garden. There is a small copse, a little to one side, that lends its shade to a cool patch of grass, several paths cross it, it can be a very pleasant spot. I know the garden from long ago, and when I was a little tired of the fete, I made for the little copse of trees. No sooner had I set foot under them than I saw a large lady coming toward me from the other direction; her size almost alarmed me, there was no one else around at all for me to compare her, but I was still convinced that I didn't know any women she wasn't taller than by a head and shoulders—in my initial consternation, I thought by several. But as I neared her, I was relieved. Isabella, my old friend! "How did you get out of your stables?" "Oh, it wasn't so difficult, they only keep me on out of kindness, my time is past, I tell my gentleman that instead of standing around uselessly in the stable I'd like to see a bit of the world while I have the strength, and if I say that to my gentleman, he understands, he fishes out some garments belonging to the late lamented, helps me slip them on, and lets me go with his blessings." "How lovely you look!" I said, not quite truthfully, nor quite mendaciously either […]

Scenes from the Defense of a Farm

There was a simple wooden fence, almost head height, and with no gaps in it. Behind it stood three men whose faces one could see over the top of the fence, the one in the middle was the tallest, the two flanking him were both more than a head shorter. Pressed up against him, they made a solid group. These three men were defending the fence, or rather the whole farmyard it enclosed. There were other men present as well, but they were not directly involved in the defense. One was sitting at a little table in the middle of the yard; it being a warm day, he had taken off his tunic and hung it over the arm of the chair. He had in front of him a number of small pieces of paper and in large expansive characters that used up a lot of ink was writing on them. From time to time he looked at a small plan that was tacked onto the table farther up, it was a drawing of the courtyard, and the man—the commander—was drawing up orders for the defense on the basis of the plan. Sometimes he would half stand up to look to the three defenders and across the fence into the open country. What he saw there also played into the orders he was writing. He was working hastily, as the tense situation demanded. A small barefooted boy who was playing in the sand nearby would deliver the little notes when they were finished and when the commander called him. But each time the commander first had to clean the boy's hands, dirty as they were from the wet sand, on his own tunic before giving him the notes. The sand was wet from water from a large tub in which a man was washing the soldiers' shirts, he had also strung up a clothesline that ran from a lath in the fence to a spindly linden tree that stood in the middle of the yard. Some laundry had been hung up to dry on this, and when the commander suddenly took off the shirt that had been sticking to his sweaty body, pulled it over his head and with a curt shout tossed it to the man by the tub, the latter took one of the dry shirts off the line and handed it to him. In the shade of a tree not far from the tub sat a young man rocking on a chair, unconcerned with everything going on around him, his gaze drifting around to the sky and the flights of birds, practicing military signals on a bugle. It was as needful now as anything else, but sometimes it got to be too much for the commander, who, without looking up from his task, motioned to the bugler to desist, and when that didn't help he turned and shouted at him, and then there was silence for a while, till the bugler experimentally began to blow again and, getting carried away, gradually increased his volume to the previous level. The curtains of the gable window were drawn, nothing unusual about that, since all the windows on that side of the house were somehow covered to protect them from the sight and the attack of the enemy, only behind that particular curtain there cowered the daughter of the farmer, looking down at the bugler, and the sounds of his playing so enraptured her that sometimes the only way she could take them in was with her eyes closed and her hand on her breast. Her rightful place was actually in the hall of the back building supervising the maids who were plucking lint for bandages, but she hadn't been able to endure it there, where the sounds reached her only dimly, never satisfactorily, only arousing her yearning, and she had crept through the dead abandoned house up here. Sometimes she leaned out a little to see that her father was still at his work and hadn't by chance gone off to inspect the domestics, because then she would not have been able to stay up here a moment longer. No, he was still there, smoking his pipe, on the stone steps to the house, carving wooden shingles, a great pile of which, finished and half-finished, as well as the pieces of wood from which they were carved, lay about him. The house and the roof would unfortunately suffer from the impending battle, and it was necessary to plan ahead. From the window beside the front door, which, apart from a small chink, had been boarded up, there came noise and smoke, that was the kitchen, and the farmer's wife was just putting the finishing touches to lunch with the army cooks. The great range was not enough for this, two further cauldrons had been set up, but, as it turned out, they were not enough either:

it being very important to the commander to have his troops plentifully fed. Therefore, the decision had been taken to set up a third cauldron as well, but as this one was slightly damaged, a man on the garden side of the house had been set to solder it. He had originally begun doing this in front of the house, but the commander had been unable to tolerate the noise of the hammering, and the cauldron had had to be trundled away. The cooks were terribly impatient, they kept sending someone along to check whether the cauldron had been finished yet, but it wasn't, and wouldn't be in time for today's lunch, and they would have to tighten their belts a little. The commander was served first. Even though he had repeatedly and insistently said that he wanted no special arrangements, the lady of the house had been unwilling to give him the same as everyone else, nor did she want to entrust serving him to anyone else, so she pulled on a fine white apron, set a plate of strong chicken broth on a silver tray, and took it out to the commander in the yard, since it could hardly be expected of him that he would interrupt his work to go into the house and eat. He rose straightaway, impeccably polite when he saw the farmer's wife approach, but had to tell her he had no time to eat, nor peace of mind neither, but she pleaded with him with head inclined, tears welling up in her upward gazing eyes, and so succeeded in getting the commander, still standing, with a smile to take a spoonful of soup from the bowl she was yet holding in her hands. But, with that, politeness had had its due, the commander bowed and sat down to work, he probably barely sensed that the woman remained standing next to him a while, and then, sighing, returned to the kitchen. It was a different story with the appetite of the troops. No sooner had the wildly bearded face of one of the cooks appeared at the kitchen window to give the signal with a whistle that lunch was served, than everything sprang to life, much more than was welcome to the commander. From a wooden barn two men towed a handcart that was basically a glorified tub on wheels, into which the soup was poured in a broad stream from the kitchen window for the men who were not able to leave their places, and who therefore had to have their lunch brought to them. First the little wagon was trundled across to the defenders by the fence, as would probably have happened even without the commander pointing with his finger for this to be done, for those three men were presently the most exposed to the enemy, and even common soldiers knew enough to respect that, perhaps in fact more even than an officer, but above all the commander was interested in expediting the serving and keeping the disruption to his military preparations to a minimum, seeing for himself how the three, in other respects model soldiers, now concerned themselves more with the little wagon and the yard than with the scene beyond the fence. They were quickly supplied from the barrel, which was then towed along the length of the fence, because every twenty yards or so there were groups of three hunkered at the foot of the fence, ready, if required, to stand up like our first three and face the enemy. In the meantime, from inside the house, the reservists came out to the kitchen window in a long line, each man with his bowl in his hand. The bugler too approached, to the regret of the farmer's daughter, who now returned to her maids, pulling out his bowl from under his chair and stowing away his bugle in its place. And at the top of the linden tree a rustling set up, because a soldier was perched there to observe the enemy with field glasses and who in spite of his essential, indispensable work had been forgotten by the driver of the soup wagon, at least temporarily. This was the bitterer for him as a few of the men, idlers of reservists, the better to enjoy their lunch, had clustered around the foot of his tree, and the savory steam from their soup was tickling his nostrils. He didn't dare raise a shout but laid about him up in the crown of the tree, and several times jabbed down through the foliage with his telescope to draw attention to himself. All in vain. He was one of the clients of the little wagon and had to wait for it to come to him at the end of its tour. This took a long time, because the yard was extensive, with probably forty sets of three sentries to feed, and by the time the little wagon, drawn by the overtired soldiers, finally reached the linden tree there was little left in the barrel, and almost no pieces of meat. Now the lookout took what there was willingly enough when it was passed up to him in a bowl on the end of a bill-hook, but then he lost his footing on the trunk, and—some thanks—landed a kick right in the face of the man who had served him. He, in turn, understandably furious, had himself hoisted up by a comrade, and in no time he was up in the tree and now began a fight, invisible from below, that found expression in the swaying of the branches, dull groans, and flying hand-fuls of leaves, till finally the glass fell to the ground and there was immediate quiet. The commander, some-what distracted by other events—there were develop-ments afoot out in the field—happily had remarked nothing when the soldier clambered down, amicably the glass was passed back up to the lookout, and every-thing was quiet again, even the soup was not greatly depleted, as the lookout had taken the trouble before the fight broke out to secure the bowl in a windproof position in the topmost twigs.

Why are you accusing me, you bad man? I don't know you, I've never seen you before. You claim to have given me money to buy you confectionery in this shop here? I'm afraid you are certainly mistaken. You never gave me any money. Are you sure you're not confusing me with my friend Fritz? He looks nothing like me. You don't scare me by threatening to bring it up in front of the teacher. He knows me and won't believe your accusation. And my parents will certainly not reimburse you, why on earth should they? Since I never got anything from you in the first place. And now let me go. No, you may not follow me, otherwise I'll call a policeman. Aha, so you don't want to go to the police, […]

Away from here, away! Don't tell me where you're taking me. Where is your hand, I can't find it in the dark. If I were holding it, I think you wouldn't try and lose me. Do you hear me? Are you even in this room? Perhaps you're not here. What would lure you up into the ice and fog of the north, where one wouldn't even expect to find people living. You are not here, you have slipped away from these places. But to me the question whether you are here or not is a matter of life and death.

I have buried my reason happily in my hand, I carry my head upright, but my hand is hanging down, my reason is dragging it down to the ground. Look at my small, calloused, veined, wrinkled, proud-veined, five-fingered hand, how clever of me to harbor my reason in this unlikely container. What is of particular advantage is that I have two hands. As in a children's game, I can ask myself: which hand am I holding my reason in, no one will be able to guess, because through the wrinkles in my hands, I can straightaway transfer my reason from hand to the other.

It was a very difficult task, and I was afraid I would not succeed at it. Also it was late at night, I had embarked on it far too late, I'd spent the whole afternoon playing in the alley, not said anything about it to my father, who might have been able to help me, and now they were all asleep and I was sitting over my notebook all alone. "Who will help me now?" I said quietly. "I will," said a strange man, slowly sitting down in a chair to my right along the narrow side of the table—just in the way that at my lawyer father's, the parties slump down at the side of his desk—propped his elbows on the desk and stretched his legs out into the room. It was a shock to me, but this was my teacher; he would best be able to solve the problem he himself had set me. And he nodded in confirmation of this opinion, whether amiably or snootily or ironically I wasn't able to say. But was it really my teacher? At first blush and from my overall impression of him he was, but if you went into detail, it became rather more doubtful. He had, for instance, my teacher's beard, that thin, stiff, protruding, grayish-black beard covering the top lip and the entire chin. But if you leaned forward in his direction, you had the sense of some artificial arrangement, and it did nothing to allay the suspicion that my supposed teacher leaned forward in my direction, propping his beard in his hand and offering it up to my inspection.

It is a small shop, but there is a good deal of life within it,
there is no street entrance, you need to walk through
the passageway and cross a small courtyard first, only
then do you get to the door of the shop, which has a
little board with the name of the owner hanging above
it. It is a drapery, selling some finished clothes but
specializing in unprocessed linen. For the uninitiated
party entering the shop for the first time, it is completely astounding how much linen is sold there, or,
more accurately, since one doesn't get any sort of over-
view of the state of the trade, the intensity and enthu-
siasm with which it is sold. As I say, the shop has no
street entrance, and not just that, from the courtyard
you can't see any customers enter, and yet the shop is
full of people and you keep seeing new ones arriving
and old ones leaving, and you don't know where they
go. There is deep shelving along the walls, but most of
the units are clustered around pillars that support numerous vaulted spaces. As a result, you can never tell
from any particular vantage point how many people
are in the shop, new people keep emerging from behind the pillars, and the nodding of heads, the lively
gestures of hands, the shuffling of feet in the crowd,
the rustling of the material as it is spread out for inspection, the endless negotiations and arguments in
which, even if they only implicate one salesperson
and one customer, the whole shop seems to become

involved—all this seems to magnify the business way past its probable real extent. There is a wooden booth in one corner, broad, but only just high enough for a person to be seated at it, and that is the office. The plank walls must be terribly strong, the door is tiny and no one thought to put in windows, there is just one peephole, but that's kept curtained on both sides—in spite of that, it is extraordinary that anyone in this office can find enough quiet, given the noise outside, to do any writing. Sometimes the dark curtain hanging on the inside of the door is pulled aside, then one can see a small office assistant filling the entire doorway, pen stuck behind his ear and with one hand shading his eyes, looking curiously or dutifully at the pandemonium in the shop. He never takes very long, then he slips back in and lets the curtain fall shut behind him so abruptly that you can't even snatch a peep at what might be happening within. There is a certain connection between the office and the shop's till. This latter is situated just by the door to the shop and is managed by a young woman. She is kept less busy than one might have supposed. Not everyone pays cash, in fact only a small minority do, obviously there are other modes of accounting [...]

What is bothering you? What is tearing at your heart's support? What is testing your doorknob? What calls you from out on the street that won't walk in through the open gate? Oh, it's only the one you are bothering, the one at whose heart's supports you are tearing, whose doorknob you are testing, whom you are calling from the street and through whose open gate you won't walk [...]

Let me say it unambiguously: everything that is said about me is false that has as its starting point the canard that I was the first human being to befriend a horse. It is remarkable that this monstrous claim was put about and credited in the first place, still more monstrous that the matter was taken lightly, spread around and believed, and let to rest with barely a shake of the head. There is a mystery there that would be more worth investigating than whatever paltry thing I actually did. All I did was this: for twelve months I lived with a horse as a man would live with a girl he adores but who rejects him, if there were no external hindrance to do anything that might get him to his objective. I therefore locked the horse Eleanor and myself in a stable, only leaving our joint residence to give the private lessons by which I earned our keep. Unfortunately, this meant five or six hours per day, and it is by no means impossible that the loss of this time was responsible for the ultimate failure of all my endeavors, and I should like the gentlemen to whom I made appeal for the support of my enterprise and who had needed only to cough up a small amount of money for something to which I was willing to sacrifice myself the way you sacrifice a handful of oats and stuff it between the back teeth of a horse, I should like those gentlemen to hoist that on board.

A coffin had been made ready, and the carpenter loaded it onto his handcart to deliver it to the undertaker. The day was overcast and rainy. An old man emerged from the cross street and stopped before the coffin, ran his cane over it, and started a little conversation with the carpenter about the coffin industry. A woman with a shopping-bag coming down the main street bumped into the old gentleman, recognized a friend, and also stopped for a while. From the workshop the apprentice came out with a few questions to put to the master. The carpenter's wife showed her face in a window over the workshop with her new baby in her arms, and from down in the street the carpenter began to coo at the little boy, and the gentleman and the woman with the shopping bag both looked up and smiled as well. A sparrow, mistakenly supposing that it might find something edible there, had settled on the coffin and was hopping around on it. A dog sniffed at the wheels of the handcart.

There came a sudden loud knocking against the coffin lid from within. The bird flew up in panic and fluttered anxiously around the handcart. The dog barked furiously, he was the most excited of all, as though it had been his duty to predict this event, and he was inconsolable about his failure to do so. The old gentleman and his friend the shopper leapt aside and stood there with hands spread. On a sudden impulse the apprentice had leaped up onto the coffin and was sitting astride it, such a position seemed more tolerable than to wait for the coffin to open and the knocker to emerge. He may already have been regretting his impulse, but seeing as he was up there, he didn't dare dismount and all the carpenter's efforts to dislodge him were unavailing. The woman at the window, who had probably also heard the knock, but hadn't been able to trace its source and to whom it certainly hadn't occurred that it might have come from inside the coffin, understood nothing of what was happening below and looked on in bewilderment. A policeman, drawn to the spot by vague curiosity, and kept from it by vague apprehension, came dawdling up.

Then the lid was pushed open with such force that the apprentice slipped off, a quick scream followed on the part of all, the woman in the window vanished, obviously to race down the stairs with her baby. Jammed into the coffin […]

When he escaped it was nighttime. Well, the house was situated on the edge of a forest. A town house, built in a town manner, single story, bow-fronted in the urban or suburban style, with a small picket-fenced front garden, lace curtains in the windows, a town house, and yet the only dwelling far and wide. And it was a winter evening and very cold out in the open. But then it wasn't in the open, there was city traffic, because just then an electric tram came around the corner, but it wasn't the city, because the tram wasn't moving, it had been standing there forever, always in that position, as though coming around the corner. And it had been empty forever, and it was no tram, it was a wagon set up on four wheels, and in the moonlight diffusing through the fog, it could have been many things. And there was paving as in a city, the ground was laid out in slabs, an exemplarily smooth bit of paving, but it was just the dim shadows of the trees falling across the snowy country road […]

The housing department got involved, there were so many official rules, and we had neglected one of them, it turned out that a room in our apartment had to be given over to a subtenant, the case was not quite clear, and if we had punctually reported the room in question to the authorities and simultaneously stated our objections to having a tenant imposed on us, then our case might have been a strong one, but, as it was, our neglect of official paragraphs was held against us and the punishment was that we were not given any right of appeal against the decisions of the department. A disagreeable situation. The more so as the department now had the opportunity of finding us a tenant of its choosing. But we still hoped to be able to do something about that. I have a nephew who is studying law at the local university, his parents are close—though in reality very distant—relatives living in a country town, I barely know them. When the boy first moved to the capital he made himself known to us, a weak, timid, nearsighted boy with a crooked back and unpleasantly devious movements and ways of speaking. He may have a sound kernel, but we don't have the time or inclination to look that far, a boy like that, such a leggy, trembling little shoot would need no end of care and observation, which is simply beyond us, and in that case it's better not to do anything, and merely keep such a boy at a safe distance. We can give him a little support, money, advice, and in fairness we have done so already, but we have discouraged any further disagreeable and futile visits. Now, though, faced with this communication from the department, we remembered the boy. He lives somewhere up in the north of the city, certainly in pretty reduced circumstances and his board will hardly be enough to keep that weedy little body going. What about taking him in with us? Not just out of pity, we could and perhaps should have done it long ago out of pity, so not just out of pity, but we don't need it to be counted among our indubitable good points, we would be richly rewarded if at the last moment our little nephew saved us from the diktat of our housing department, appearing as some perfectly random stranger insisting on his rights. So far as we have managed to ascertain, this would be a distinct possibility. If we were able to point to a poor student to the housing department, if we could prove that this student through the loss of his room would lose not just a room but the very thing that underwrote his existence, if finally (the nephew will not refuse his part in this little performance, we will make sure of that) we could establish that he has been living at least temporarily in this room, and only moved out to his parents in the country during the admittedly long period when he was preparing for his exams—if all this were to be successfully encompassed, then our worries would be as good as over. First of all, then, we must collect the nephew, but with a car that's no trouble, we'll pick up this boy who won't know what's happened to him […]

I went abroad to live among foreigners. I hung my coat on a nail, no one looked after me. I was left alone, it was understood that I posed no danger. What can one man do against a great crowd anyway. I was there, and people left me the responsibility for my decision. I had probably been forced to it, I had needed some refuge, that will have been the tacit assumption. The further assumption was that I wouldn't be able find such a refuge, people could see how poorly I could assimilate myself, conditions there would be too alien, I was out of place. But all that was hardly given to me to feel, people were far too occupied with their own affairs, perhaps with my particular gifts and experience I could even be useful to them, but I didn't dare to intervene and they in turn didn't dare to involve me, the danger that in my strangeness I would make a mess of something was simply too great.

*I have—who else may speak so freely of his gifts—the con-*tented and indefatigable wrist of an old fisherman. Picture me sitting at home before going out fishing and marveling at it as I turn my right hand this way and that. It's enough on its own to reveal to my sight and sense the outcome of a future fishing expedition, often down to the last detail. I can see the water of my angling spot, the particular current and the particular hour, a cross section of the stream reveals itself to me, and the fish, unmistakable in number and kind; I seem to see ten, twenty, even a hundred different spots on the river in cross section, and I know just how to hold the rod, there are some that with impunity butt through the imaginary line with their heads, then I dangle my hook in front of them and already I have them on my line—the brevity of the moment of destiny charms me as I sit at my table—other fish thrust forward as far as their bellies, and I must hurry, some I am still able to capture, others get past the dangerous line tail and all and for the moment they are lost to me, although only for the moment, because to a real angler no fish is ever really lost.

When one night the small mouse that in the mouse world was loved as no other came under the blade and with a scream gave up her life for a piece of bacon, all the mice in their holes all around were taken by a trembling and shaking; their eyes blinking uncontrollably, they looked at one another in turn, while their tails in terrible agitation swept across the floor this way and that. Finally, reluctantly, they came forth, one pushing the other, all drawn to the place of death. There lay the dear little thing, in its neck the steel blade, the pink legs flattened, the feeble body frozen, to which a morsel of bacon would have been so welcome. There stood the parents, eyeing what was left of their child.

In our house, that massive building on the outskirts of town, a tenement block built around some indestructible medieval ruins, on this cold and foggy winter's morning the following appeal was put up.

To all my fellow inhabitants:

I own five toy rifles hanging on five hooks in my wardrobe. One of them is mine, I invite offers for the other four, if there are more than four interested parties, then those more than four will be asked to bring along their own rifles and leave them in my wardrobe. We need a proper basis, without a proper basis we will get nowhere. My rifles are of no practical use, the mechanism is broken, the corks are lost, only the hammer still clicks. It will not be difficult to get hold of more such rifles if necessary. But I will be happy even if fellows come forward without rifles, and at least to begin with, those of us with rifles can take them in our midst if it comes to that. This was a fighting formation that proved itself with the early American settlers against the Indians, and why should it not come in useful here, where circumstances are similar. In the long run, rifles are not essential. Even my five rifles are not essential, but seeing as they exist and I have them, they may as well be used. If the next four are unwilling to carry them, then never mind. Then as commander I alone will be armed. But we don't want a leader and so I too will either break or cast aside my rifle.

That was the first appeal. In our building no one has the time or inclination to read or even think about such appeals. Before long the little notices were awash in the stream of dirt that ran down from the attic, fed by all the corridors, swilling down the stairs and there fighting the current that came up from below. Then a week later, there was a second announcement.

My fellow dwellers!

To date no one has reported to me. When not required to earn my living, I was in the house all the time, and while I was away—keeping the door to my room open—there was on my desk a sheet of paper, on which anyone who had wanted to could have written down their names. It seems no one has done so.

When I got home at night, I found in the middle of the room a good-sized, really an outsize egg. It was almost as high as the table and accordingly curved. It wobbled gently this way and that. I was terribly curious, gripped it between my knees and carefully cut it open with my pocketknife. It was already fertilized. Crumpling, the shell fell apart and out leapt a still unfledged stork-like bird beating the air with its too-short wings. "What are you doing in our world?" I wanted to ask it, kneeling down in front of it and gazing into its frightened blinking eyes. But it left me and hopped away half-fluttering along the walls as though it had sore feet. "We can help each other," I thought; I unpacked my supper on the table and beckoned to the bird, which was just drilling into a couple of my books with its beak. He came right away, sat down on a chair, evidently he was a little house-trained already, with whistling breath he sniffed at the slice of sausage I had set down in front of him, only to spike it with his beak and flip it back to me. "My mistake," I thought, "it stands to reason you don't take something just emerged from its egg and offer it sausage. A woman's hand would have been helpful at this stage." And I looked at it sharply to see if it might be possible to intuit its favored diet. "If," it occurred to me, "if it comes from the stork family, then it will be wanting fish. Well, I am prepared to provide fish. Albeit not for nothing. My income will hardly permit me to keep a domestic bird. If I am to make such a sacrifice, then I will expect in return a life-enhancing service of equal value. He is a stork, so once he is full grown on my fish, why doesn't he take me with him to southern climes. I have long desired to go there, and the only reason I haven't is want of storks' wings" So I took out paper and ink, into which I dunked the bird's beak, and experiencing no resistance from the bird, wrote as follows: "I, stork-like bird, in the event that you provide me with fish, frogs, and worms" (these last two items I wrote down purely on conventional grounds) "till I am fully fledged, do hereby undertake to carry you on my back to southern climes." Then I wiped its beak and held the paper in front its eyes for approval, before folding it up and stowing it in my briefcase. Then straightaway I went out for fish; on this occasion I was obliged to pay the full price, but the fishmonger promised to keep spoilt fish and an abundance of worms for me at a discount. Perhaps the voyage to southern climes would turn out to be a bargain after all. And I was delighted to observe the bird's appetite. With gurgles, the fish went down and filled the pinkish belly. Day after day, not at all like human infants, the bird made progress in his development. Admittedly, the reek of rotten fish never left my room, nor was it easy to find and remove the waste of the bird on each occasion, and also the winter season and the price of coal prohibited the highly needful airing out of the place—what did it matter, come spring I would be swimming through the lightsome air to the gleaming southland. Its wings grew, acquired a covering of feathers, its muscles strengthened, finally it was time to embark on some trial flights. Regrettably, there was no mother stork handy, and despite the bird's willingness to learn, my own teaching would probably not be sufficient. But evidently he knew enough to see that by concentrating on me and paying close attention he could make up for the deficiencies in my tuition. We began with the chair flight. I got up, he followed, I jumped down with outspread arms, he fluttered after. Later we progressed to the table, and finally to the wardrobe: all our flights were systematically repeated many times.

*Conventional accounts of world history often fail us com-*pletely, and human intuition often leads one astray, but it does take one somewhere, and doesn't desert one. Hence the traditional report of the Seven Wonders of the World has always been accompanied by a rumor that there was also an eighth, and of this eighth there were various possibly contradictory accounts, their uncertainty being accounted for by references to the dim and distant past.

You don't have to leave the house. Stay at your desk and listen. Or don't even listen, wait for it to bother you. Don't even wait, be completely quiet and alone. The world will offer itself to you to be unmasked, it cannot do otherwise, it will writhe in front of you in ecstasies.

"Ladies and gentlemen," thus the address of the Arab in Western clothes to the group of tourists who barely heard him but gazed, stunned by wonder, at the extraordinary construction that loomed up in front of them from the cold stone floor, "you will admit that my firm far outperforms all other tour operators, even those with venerable reputations, and rightly so. While these competitors, in the old and slipshod manner, show their clients the seven wonders of the world, our firm shows the eighth."

We have all heard tell of Red Peter—half the world has.
But when he came to perform in our town, I decided
I would get to know him personally. It's surprisingly
easy to gain access to him. In the great cities where
the whole world clamors, cannily, to be admitted to
see the great celebrities breathing in close proximity,
there may be certain difficulties; here, where people
are content to remain in their seats and gawp at remarkable things from gawping distance, I was, as the
hotel porter told me, the only one so far to have an-
nounced a visit. The impresario, one Herr Busenau,
received me cordially. I hadn't expected to see such a
modest, almost insignificant-looking fellow. He was
sitting in Red Peter's anteroom, eating a custard pudding. Although it was still morning, he was already
in the tails he wore to performances. No sooner did
he catch sight of me, the insignificant, unknown visitor, than he leapt up, the owner of lofty distinctions,
the king of animal tamers, the holder of honorary
degrees from the great universities—leapt up, shook
me warmly by the hand, bade me sit down, wiped his
spoon on the tablecloth, and graciously offered it to
me that I might finish his custard pudding. He refused
to accept my polite refusal and set about feeding me
himself. It was all I could do to push him away with
plate and spoon. "It's so nice of you to have come," he
said to me in a marked accent, "very nice indeed. Also,

you've come at the right time, it's an unfortunate thing
that Red Peter isn't always up to visits, he's often loath
to see people; at such times no one can be admitted, regardless of who they are, even I, even I myself am only
allowed to visit him on a business basis, so to speak, on
the stage. Then straight after the performance I have
to disappear, while he goes home alone, locks himself
up in his room, and usually stays there till the following evening. He always has a large basket of fruit in his
room, and that keeps him going during such episodes.
Naturally, I never leave him entirely unsupervised; I
am careful to take the apartment opposite, and I watch
him from behind drawn curtains."

"*As I sit opposite you like this, Red Peter, listen to you speak,*
raise a glass to you, really—I don't mind whether you
take it as a compliment or not, it's the plain truth—I
quite forget that you're a chimpanzee. It's only by and
by, as I find my way back to reality from my thoughts,
that my eyes show me whose visitor I actually am."

"Yes."

"You've gone so quiet, why is that? Only a moment
ago, you were sharing with me your astoundingly per-
tinent views of our town, and now so quiet."

"Quiet?"

"Is something the matter? Should I call your
trainer? Perhaps you're accustomed to having a meal
at this time?"

"No, no. Everything's all right. I can tell you what
the matter was. Sometimes I feel such an antipathy
to humans that I am close to vomiting. Of course, it's
nothing to do with the individual, or your gracious
presence. It's directed against the species as a whole.
Nor is there anything unusual about this, for instance
if you'd been in the habit of living with apes, I'm sure
you would have such spasms as well, for all your self-
control. And it's not so much the smell of humans that
so disgusts me as the human smell I have taken on
myself, and that is mingled with the smell of my old
homeland. Here, smell it yourself! On my chest! Dig
your nose deeper into my pelt! Deeper, I tell you."

"I'm afraid I don't have a terribly acute sense of smell. I seem to pick up the usual smell of a cared-for body, nothing beyond that. Admittedly, the noses of city dwellers are not representative. I expect you can smell thousands of things that pass us by."

"Used to, sir, used to. It's different now."

"Since you've broached the topic, might I ask: how long is it that you have been living among us?"

"Five years now. On August 5, it will have been five years."

"Extraordinary. To throw off your simian origins and in the space of five years to have galloped through the whole of human evolution. No one can have done that before you. In that regard, you surely have the field to yourself."

"I know it's a lot, and sometimes it feels like more than I can deal with. In my calmer hours I don't view things as exuberantly. Do you know how I came to be captured?"

"I've read everything that's been published about you. You received a wound from a gunshot and were taken prisoner."

"Yes. In fact, I was shot at twice, once here in my cheek, of course the wound was much bigger than the scar is now, and a second time in the hip. Let me pull down my trousers and show you the place. The bullet hit me like this, and that was the more serious wound, I fell out of my tree, and when I came around I was in steerage in a cage."

"In steerage! In a cage! One takes a different view of such events, hearing you relate them."

"And it's different again if one has experienced them, sir. Till that point I hadn't known what that means: to have no way out. This was no four-sided cage with bars, there were only three walls, and they were made fast to a chest, the chest constituted the fourth wall. The whole thing was so low to the ground that I was unable to stand up, and so narrow that I couldn't sit down with my legs extended. All I could do was squat there with my knees pressed against me. In my rage I couldn't bear to see anyone, and I remained facing the chest, hunkered there for days and nights with knees trembling while the bars cut into my back. This sort of accommodation for wild animals is approved for the early days, and with my experience I can't deny that from the human perspective there's something to it. But what did I care about the human perspective in those days? I was facing the chest: rip away the planks, bite a hole in them, squeeze yourself through a chink that in reality is barely wide enough to be looked through, and whose aspect the first time you saw it was enough for you to greet it with a blissful howl of incomprehension. Where do you want to go? The world begins beyond the boards."

The struggle began. My two hands clapped shut the book I had been reading and pushed it aside so that it didn't get in the way. They saluted me and hailed me as their referee. Then the fingers were grappling with one another, and the hands began their scuttling along the table edge, now right now left, depending on which was prevailing. I did not take my eyes off them. If they are my hands, I must be a fair referee, otherwise I'll be guilty of a miscarriage of justice. But my job is not an easy one, both palms take advantage of the dark for various bits of skullduggery that I must not overlook, so I press my chin down on the tabletop, and from now on nothing escapes my notice. All my life, without my having anything against the left, I have favored the right. If the left at any point had complained, I would—fair-minded and conciliatory as I am—promptly have put an end to the abuse. But it didn't make a murmur and merely hung down at my side; while the right might be exuberantly doffing my hat on the street, the left timidly bumped against my thigh. That was no sort of preparation for the battle that was now commencing. Little left wrist, how will you seek to prevail against the mighty right? How assert your girlish digits in the grip of those five others? This isn't a fair fight, more the ruthless extinction of the left. Already it's been driven back to the table's far corner, with the right pounding against it rhythmically like the piston of a machine. If in this dire emergency I hadn't had the saving idea that these are my own hands that are fighting and that it's possible for me with a slight jerk to pull them apart, and hence put an end to their fight and their extremity—if I hadn't happened to have that thought, then the left would have been snapped off at the wrist and thrown off the table and the right, with the immoderateness of the victor, would have driven up into my watching face like the five-headed hound of hell itself. Instead of which, behold them now, lying peaceably together, the right stroking the back of the left, and I, the dishonest referee, complaisantly nodding.

Sweet snake, why so distant, come closer, even closer, there, enough, stay there. Oh, you have no discipline. How am I to have mastery over you when you are so undisciplined. It will be a difficult job. Let me begin by asking you to curl up. Curl up, I said, and you stretch out. Don't you understand me? You don't. I am talking to you plainly: curl up. No, you don't understand. So, I'll demonstrate it to you with my stick. First you must describe a large circle, then a second inside the first, and so on. If you are still holding your head up, then lower it slowly to the melody of the flute I will play later, and when I stop, then you too stop, with your head in the middle of the innermost circle.

The great swimmer! the people called. The great swimmer!
I was coming from the Olympics in the city of X, where
I had obtained a world record in swimming. I stood on
the steps of the station of my native town—which is
it now?—and gazed down at the crowd, indistinct in
the evening sun. A girl whose cheek I dandled swiftly
draped a cloak over me that said in some foreign lan-
guage: for the Olympic champion. A car drew up and
several gentlemen made me get in, two gentlemen accompanied me, the mayor and someone else. In no
time we were in a festive hall, a choir was singing up
in a gallery as I stepped in, all the guests, several hundred of them, rose to their feet and chanted something
I couldn't quite make out. On my left was a minister,
I don't know why when he introduced himself I was
so alarmed by the word, I eyed him up and down in
panic before coming to my senses, on my right was the
wife of the mayor, a well-endowed lady indeed, everything about her, especially at chest height, seemed to
be bristling with roses and peacock feathers. Opposite
me was a man with a strikingly pale face, I missed his
name when we were introduced, he had set his elbows
down on the table—he had been awarded an unusual
amount of space—and stared into space, he did not
speak, and on either side of him were two beautiful
fair-haired girls who seemed to be in a good mood and
had no end of things to say, so that I didn't know which

of them to look at. Beyond that, in spite of the lavish lighting, I couldn't make out who was there, perhaps because the scene was in continual motion, servants were running here and there serving food, toasts were drunk, perhaps there was even too much illumination. Also, there was a certain amount of disorder—though in no way excessive—because some of the guests, ladies especially, were sitting with their backs to the table and in such a way, furthermore, that not the backs of their chairs but their actual backs grazed the table. I pointed out this fact to the girls opposite, but—though so talkative otherwise—they didn't have anything to say about it, just looked at me and smiled. When a bell gave the signal—the servants stopped where they were between the rows of chairs—the fat man opposite me got up and gave a speech. I only wonder why the man was so sad! During his speech, he continually mopped his face with his handkerchief, which might have been understandable in view of his bulk and the heat of the room and the strain of giving a speech, but I distinctly noticed that the whole thing was a subterfuge intended to conceal the fact that he was wiping tears from his eyes. After he had finished, I of course stood up and gave a rejoinder. I felt positively compelled to, because there were a few things here and for all I knew elsewhere as well that seemed to call for a clear and public explanation, for which reason I began:

Respected guests! It may have come to your attention that I hold a world record, but if you were to ask me how I came by it, I would have no satisfactory reply. You see, I can't really swim at all. I always wanted to learn, but I never had an occasion to. So how come I was sent by my country to participate in the Olympic Games? A question that preoccupies me too. To begin with, I must tell you that this is not my fatherland, and try as I may, I cannot understand a word of what is spoken here. The most obvious explanation would be some mix-up, but there is no mix-up, I hold the record, I went home, my name is what it is said to be, everything so far is true, but beyond that point nothing is true, I am not in my homeland, I do not know you and cannot understand you. Now something else that not exactly—but at least diffusely—repudiates the idea of a mix-up: it doesn't greatly bother me that I don't understand you, nor does it greatly seem to bother you that you don't understand me. All I took from the previous speaker's speech was that it was terribly sad, but not only is this knowledge enough for me, it is in fact too much. And this is how things stand with every conversation I have had since my arrival here. But to get back to my world record […]

A legend is an attempt to explain the inexplicable; emerging as it does from a basis of truth, it is bound to end in the inexplicable.

We have four legends concerning Prometheus. According to the first of them, for betraying the gods to mankind, he was shackled to a peak in the Caucasus, and the gods sent eagles that ate at his liver as it kept growing back.

According to the second, the pain of the jabbing beaks drove Prometheus ever deeper into the rocks until he became one with them.

According to the third, his betrayal was forgotten in the course of millennia, the gods forgot, the eagles forgot, he himself forgot.

According to the fourth, everyone grew tired of the procedure that had lost its raison d'être. The gods grew tired, the eagles. Even the wound grew tired and closed.

The real riddle was the mountains.

Afterword

Franz Kafka is the master of the literary fragment. In no other European author does the proportion of completed and published works loom quite so ... small in the overall mass of his papers, which consist largely of broken-off beginnings. The prose works that Kafka viewed as finished and which he submitted for publication take up perhaps 350 pages of print, barely a tenth of the whole oeuvre (if one includes the diaries, which contain numerous literary efforts). This is to leave out of account those hundreds of manuscript pages that Kafka personally destroyed or whose destruction he ordered, as well as the numerous notebooks from his final year, whose fate remains a matter of speculation today.

The fragile, fragmentary quality of Kafka's work has had interestingly divergent consequences: on the one hand, it has presented editors and readers with considerable difficulties; on the other, it has caused us to begin to take the literary fragment seriously. World literature is inconceivable without Kafka's best-known work, *The Trial*—there are adaptations of it in film and as graphic novel—and in both plot and nightmarish atmosphere, *The Trial* has affected millions of readers to the degree that the book is hardly any longer considered as what it is: a fragment. Moreover, we have come to accept that there can be such a thing as a completed masterly fragment. Kafka's three novels, none of them finished, have played no small part in this development.

But what do we do with all the other writing? What is the adequate form for the publication and reception of a work that consists of beginnings of all lengths? Kafka's friend and first editor, Max Brod, tried to resolve the problem by taking a hand himself, supplying his own titles and cutting away incomprehensible material—all with the aim of presenting actual "works" and of rescuing Kafka from the stigma of a failed author. This is not the way one would proceed nowadays. So, in 1982, S. Fischer Verlag embarked on a critical edition in which every recorded sentence of Kafka's is presented in its original context, regardless of whether the author endorsed it as publishable, rewrote it, broke off after a few words, or simply deleted it. Not only the major manuscript notebooks were submitted to this process, but so was every single page, even small notebooks filled with pencil scribblings, even single scraps of paper, whose place in the chronology had to be found. The twelve volumes of this critical edition (there is a volume of letters still to come) has served as a dependable basis for all further editions of single works as well as of all new translations.

As an edition, this is a considerable advance, because with it we can, as never before, see Kafka in his entirety. But critical editions address themselves to, shall we say, a limited readership. Academic presentation and generally dry-as-dust philological commentaries scare off the lover of literature, who is looking for something to "merely" read and enjoy, not to study the texts or learn in detail of their genesis. A critical edition is indeed capable of launching new waves of reception—especially if it comes with surprising discoveries—but it still needs general editions for non-academic readers to spread these discoveries and make them available to a wider readership.

It must be said that Kafka's fragments offer considerable resistance to such an undertaking. They require of the reader that she negotiate a vast number of texts of every length and form, without the aid of a familiar title, say, or an order established by the author—and, yes, in many cases it's not even clear whether a text was broken off or viewed by Kafka as finished.

Kafka's unpublished stories and the compilation of short and very short fragments take up two large volumes of the Fischer edition totalling some 1,100 pages (*Nachgelassene Schriften und Fragmente*, volumes I and II, first published in 1992 and 1993), with each volume accompanied by a further volume of textual variants and commentary. These are literary treasure houses whose fullness, when one browses through them, is simply astounding, because aside from the novels—which of course are in their separate volumes—they contain everything that the term *fragment* can offer:

from the flash of an idea that doesn't even take up a complete sentence, to a pantomimically sketched scene, to a substantial and almost achieved story.

There is a plenitude that is hard to master and that in and of itself becomes intractable: the reader will run into some jewel, and not find it again without long seeking. Indexes or other editorial aids are mostly inapplicable to these texts, and the paperback editions that merely cut away the variants and commentaries didn't change that. Hence, decades after their first publication, Kafka's fragments have remained terra incognita, even for the majority of his German readers.

The difficulties and obstacles when it comes to the translation of such chaotic material are comparable. While there are innumerable renderings of classic Kafka tales like *Metamorphosis*, there have only been a very few, mostly half-hearted attempts at presenting the unpublished fragments in other languages. As a result, we have Kafka as a major twentieth-century author in many languages—even as reading for school-children—but what readers see in all these languages is only the tip of the iceberg, with its gigantic base obscured from sight. Kafka's fragments are literally "lost" to all these readers and will probably remain so for years to come.

The situation in English is no better. In 1954, Schocken Books issued a now out-of-print volume, *Dearest Father: Stories and Other Writings*, edited by Max Brod and translated by Ernst Kaiser and Eithne Wilkins. Alongside Kafka's "Letter to his Father," this volume actually contains no complete "stories," only "other writings" in the form of notes, fragments, and aphorisms. This was the first, and for a long time the only attempt to allow the English-speaking reader access to Kafka's workshop. In 2012, Sun Vision Press published Ida Pfitzner's translation of the complete volume I of the *Nachgelassene Schriften und Fragmente*, under the title *Abandoned Fragments*. The far longer volume II—containing Kafka's later writings, from 1916 to 1924—has yielded a few individual translations of prominent pieces, particularly the unfinished story "The Burrow" and the Zürau Aphorisms, but the great majority of the pieces have been neglected for decades and remain practically unknown.

The present edition offers a representative selection from volume II of the *Nachgelassene Schriften* in Michael Hofmann's translation. The selection seeks above all to be accessible: these texts are highly approachable, "readable" pieces—not mere linguistic shards or variants, but substantive texts giving a sense of the enormous array of literary forms of which Kafka was such a great master.

In addition, our volume contains some twenty pages of texts by the younger Kafka that have lately appeared in the *Abandoned Fragments* volume. In this way, the reader is not restricted to discoveries from the later Kafka, but is offered a tour of the great fragmentarian in every epoch.

REINER STACH, JULY 2020

Index of first lines

I can swim as well as the others, only I have a better memory than they do, so I have been unable to forget my formerly not being able to swim. Since I have been unable to forget it, being able to swim doesn't help me, and I can't swim after all.

* * *

A delicate matter, this tiptoeing across a crumbling board set down as a bridge, nothing underfoot, having to scrape together with your feet the ground you are treading on, walking on nothing but your reflection down in the water below, holding the world together with your feet, your hands cramping at the air to survive this ordeal.

* * *

"You are forever speaking of death, and not dying."

"And yet die I shall. I am just intoning my swan song. One person's song is longer, another's shorter. The only difference is a few words."